BECOMING MARILYN

Alex McGilvery

Becoming Marilyn

Alex McGilvery

Copyright © 2018 by Alex McGilvery

For information contact:
http://alexmcgilvery.com

ISBN 978-1-989092-10-1

Acknowledgements

I have the privilege of knowing many transgender people in all walks of life. This isn't their story. They each have their own and they are all different.

Marilyn is a fictional character who burst onto the scene in *Sarcasm is my Superpower*. She wanted her own book, so here it is. Don't take my word for what a transgender person experiences, go listen to their story.

- 1 -

"It all started with Ophelia. Robert died when I put on that dress and looked in the mirror and saw Marilyn for the first time. Well, maybe I knew something before her, but she brought it to the surface."

Marilyn looked at Dr. Tripp, but he just looked back at her with those damned blue eyes seeing past all the lies and excuses. Not that Dr. Tripp did anything as crass as challenge her. He expected her to do it for herself.

"Grade six," Marilyn said, "Mr. Telfer taught us bits and pieces of English literature. He decided we should act out a scene from a play in Shakespeare. We chose groups of four. My group consisted of Mack, Joe and Tom, plus me. We were *Smells like Rock and Roll.* I played drums. We probably sucked, but we had fun."

Dr. Tripp nodded. Marilyn took a deep breath. She could do this. She'd lived through it; it shouldn't be hard to tell the story.

"We met in the clubhouse after school. We'd built it in the wood lot from scavenged lumber. Mack had the scripts Mr. Telfer handed out.

'I'll be Hamlet,' Mack bossed everything. He played lead guitar and I remember him as being amazing, perhaps he was. 'Joe you be Claudius and Tom can be Polonius. Robert, you're Ophelia, because you've got the hair for it.'

I had long hair because all the drummers I watched did. My dad rolled his eyes, but let me grow it out. The others had buzz cuts, but I never heard any of them complain they wanted any different.

I looked at the script and saw Ophelia was a girl. I wanted to argue, but you didn't argue with Mack. The other guys were snickering at me, but Mack asked which of them wanted Ophelia and they shut up. We were twelve, and girls were a different species. We might watch them, even admire them, but we weren't going to hang out with them. That's why we met in a crooked little shack in the woods, because the girls wouldn't go there.

'Learn your parts,' Mack said when it got time to go home for supper.

Next day we met again. We hung out there every day, the only thing different was we practiced Hamlet instead of music. Yeah, we rehearsed out there. I had a drum set cobbled together from garbage cans and I used stakes from our croquet game as drumsticks. Mack had a real guitar. Joe played this tiny piano. It sounded terrible, but he acted like he was a maestro on it. Tom filled in on whatever Mack told him to use. We must have sounded awful, but out in those woods no one cared. Mack would look at me and say *Just keep the beat.*"

"Ophelia?" Dr. Tripp said.

Marilyn swallowed and took a sip from her water bottle.

"It was the scene with *to be or not to be* and Mack had memorized the whole thing. He stomped around the clubhouse putting us in place.

'I told you to learn your parts." None of the rest of us had bothered. We read through the scene. Mack made us go back and read with feeling. He did the same with the music. We just did what he told us, that was always easier.

'We have a week to get it together,' Mack said, 'Learn your parts.'

'I don't want to memorize all this,' Joe said. 'What good is it?'

'Do you want to be prancing about on the stage with this,' Mack flicked the script. 'in your hand? You'll look a moron and make us look bad.'

'Ok, Ok, geez,' Joe rolled his eyes.

Tom shrugged and peered at the script like he was studying it furiously and we laughed.

'Robert," Mack pointed at me, "try to sound like a girl."

'How do I do that?' I asked.

'Talk high and breathy,' Joe said, 'like my sister.'

'Talk about stupid stuff,' Tom said. 'Girls are dumb.'

I went home and listened to my Dad and Brent, my older brother, talk. They were full of opinions. Neither of them left any space for other people's ideas. They were like Mack, who talked and just assumed you'd agree with him. I tried to listen to Mom, but she didn't say much. I helped her with the dishes.

'I'm in this play thing at school," I said as I dried the plates. 'I have to play the part of Ophelia. She's a girl in Hamlet. Mack told me I had to talk like a girl.'

'Playing a girl might be hard,' Mom handed me another plate.

'It's just a stupid play.'

'Well,' Mom's soapy hands paused in the water. 'If you want to be really simple about it; girls talk like they care about people. Boys talk like they care about ideas.'

She started up the hands again and didn't say anything more about it.

When I was going to bed, Mom came into my room carrying a white bundle.

'I thought you might want a costume." She unfolded a white dress on my bed. It looked strange in the center of all the rock posters I had up on my walls. 'It doesn't fit me anymore, but you should be able to wear it. Just try not to get it too dirty.'

She kissed me good night kind of absently and left her wedding dress on my bed. I recognized it from the pictures in our downstairs hall. I rolled it up and stuffed it in my backpack to take to school.

I spent the day eavesdropping on girls. Their conversation had a different rhythm than the boys. They didn't interrupt each other as much and it seemed to be all about other people. Mostly boys. They liked Mack, didn't like Joe and didn't even know I existed. At the clubhouse, we went through the scene. Joe and Tom sort of knew their parts I couldn't remember the words at all. Mack glared at me like he was Shakespeare and I was wrecking his play.

'I have a costume,' I said, desperate to distract him.

'So?' Mack said.

Now I had to pull out the dress and show him. Once I showed him the dress, I had to put it on. The guys laughed and joked.

'Be serious,' I said, 'This is my Mom's wedding dress.'

'For real?' Mack asked.

I just nodded. He helped me put the dress on over my pants and t-shirt.

'You need some..." Tom put his hands out in front of his chest.

'Shut it," Mack brushed my hair back away from my face and stepped back.

"I swear I saw his eyes change as I became a different species. I wasn't Robert any more but Ophelia, a girl. The other guys were pulling the usual guy teasing, but Mack didn't say anything. Terror reared up in me, worse than the time a stray dog chased me through the woods. I tore the dress off and flung it at him and ran out of the clubhouse. We ran through those woods every day of our lives. Those paths were as familiar as my own home, but I ran like I was lost. There was shouting behind me as Mack yelled at the other two.

"I was a boy, a fucking boy. I pissed standing up and made fart jokes. I didn't wear dresses, especially not wedding dresses. I smacked into a tree and fell to the ground. Whatever made me afraid didn't go away. Boys face their fears. They didn't cry, or run away. I should have kicked that dog, killed it with a stick. I was a boy. I punched the tree as hard as I could because there was no dog. A bone in my hand cracked and sent pain up my arm.

"Mack found me there, huddled on the ground, crying like a girl."

"I think that's enough for today," Dr. Tripp made a few notes.

"What?" Marilyn stopped cradling her right hand and took a sip of water. The hand ached like it had for months after she broke it.

"Why are you here, Marilyn?" He put the note pad and pen down.

"I need to do this before I can have the surgery." Marilyn winced at how close she sounded to tears.

"True," Dr. Tripp said, "the counseling is mandated before the reassignment surgery, but the goal is to help you identify who you are."

"I know who I am," Marilyn took a breath and banished the quaver in her voice.

"Then we will get along just fine," Dr. Tripp said. "I'll see you next week."

Marilyn put her water bottle in her purse and left the office. From the door of Dr. Tripp's building the water of Pugent Sound was visible in the distance. Clouds covered the mountains on the other side.

The bus took her up Madison to where she changed buses to get to the University.

The walk to the library left her both chilled and damp. October in Seattle wasn't as cold as it was back home in Punky's Hound's Corners, but Marilyn hadn't adapted to the almost constant moisture in the air. It wreaked havoc with her hair and made her unsure whether she was too hot or too cold. She pulled her sweater from her purse before she entered the library proper and put it one. The climate control to keep the books dry also meant cold.

She popped into the washroom and checked her makeup. There was little she could do with the hair but put it back in a pony-tail. A couple of touches and her make-up passed inspection. Marilyn fussed with the scarf until she felt it looked like a part of her outfit instead of like it hid something. Shit, she hated what puberty had done to her.

"Leave it for Dr. Tripp," she ordered her reflection, then went to do the reading for the Introduction to Social Work course with a paper due this week.

***

"So," Professor Dingman said, "Social work moved from being the action of women attempting to do good in poorer districts to being work directly related to increasing the capacity of the people to help themselves. We share with other professions the idea of *Do no harm,* yet unlike some professions we give value to the client's own decision. The right of the client to make their own determinations is a foundation of social work ethics."

Marilyn followed his movements from the middle of the class. The others scribbled notes, but she couldn't remember his words if she tried to write it all down. So she focused on him as he paced across the front of the class.

"What are some examples of ways in which society tries to limit a person's ability to choose?"

"Where someone lives," a black student said, "there are places my Dad could buy a house, and places he couldn't."

"Right," the professor wrote on the board, "race is an issue."

"Money is too," a girl behind Marilyn said. "You have a lot more choice if you have money than if you're poor."

"Good, class divisions."

The chalk squeaked. Marilyn's stomach ached. She didn't know if it was from the class or the session with Dr. Tripp. She hated bringing up all that stuff; it wasn't her, not anymore. Other students listed barriers to self-determination.

"Gender," Marilyn said.

"I think we have that," Professor Dingman pointed to where he'd written about how women have a more difficult time claiming their own decisions.

"No," Marilyn forced back the heat in her voice. "People are told what gender they are, and we're supposed to just live with it."

"Yes, right." The professor pointed at another hand and the discussion moved away from her. The class wrapped up and the students escaped.

"Hello," a girl said behind Marilyn. She turned and looked down at a girl with ebony skin and hair clinging to her skull like felt.

"Hi," Marilyn didn't want to step back, or sit down again, but she hated staring down at people. Maybe it was time to go back to flats. They made more sense with the amount of walking she had to do.

"I love your scarf," the girl said, "it looks like something from my country. May I?" She reached out to touch it.

"I don't like taking it off," Marilyn put her hand to her neck.

"Ok fine." Instead of being angry or leaving the girl smiled and white teeth flashed at Marilyn. "I'm supposed to wear a scarf, so I can cover my head." She pulled a scarf from her purse and demonstrated, covering up the fuzz on her skull. "I have so many scarves, but I don't wear them now. I don't have to cover my head here." She handed the scarf to Marilyn. "You wear it. We make the designs in Uganda, but here they are just designs."

"Are you sure?" The material lay soft and weightless in her hands. "At least let me buy you coffee."

"Ok," the girl said as they left the classroom. "I have time before my next class."

"This is my last class," Marilyn said, "I'm taking an extra year to do my courses."

"I'm Birungi." The girl gave Marilyn another brilliant smile.

"Marilyn." They walked into the hall and sat at a table. "You stay here and I'll get us coffee." Birungi nodded and sat while Marilyn went to stand in line. She returned to the table with the coffee and creamers and sugars.

"I forgot to ask how you like it." Marilyn put the tray on the table. Birungi put milk and sugar in her coffee.

"At home milk and sugar are rare." She gave Marilyn one of her quick grins, "Here they are not special, but I still like them."

They sat in silence drinking their coffee. The babble of conversations surrounded them, but didn't touch them.

"Hi, I'm Anna." Marilyn lifted her eyes to the blonde girl who had talked about women's issues in the class.

"Marilyn."

She sat down in an empty chair.

"What's it like?" she asked, "Not knowing what you are and having to decide?"

"I know who I am," Marilyn frowned at the girl.

"But you had to decide to change, right?" Anna leaned forward. "You had to take hormones to grow breasts and all that, right?"

"What I am now," Marilyn clenched her teeth, "is a woman."

"But -"

"Excuse me," Birungi put a hand on Anna's arm. "You are upsetting Marilyn, my friend."

"God, I thought from what you'd said in class you'd want to talk about it." She jumped to her feet and walked away.

"Thanks," Marilyn sipped her coffee. The dark bitter flavour eased the tightness she hadn't known was there. Birungi reached up and adjusted the scarf around Marilyn's throat.

"We all have our scars," Birungi said, "we must choose when to speak of them, or not."

-2-

"You were telling me about Ophelia," Dr. Tripp looked at her.

"I'd broken my hand on the tree," Marilyn rubbed it absently. "I didn't want to say anything. Mack walked me to my house and didn't say a word the whole time.

'Heard you're doing Shakespeare in old Telfer's class.' Brent said to me when I got in the door. Tom's brother said you were Ophelia.'

I tried to shrug it off, but Brent was four years older than me and I never won an argument against him.

'Catch the ball for me." Brent pushed the football into my gut and went outside. I threw the ball and the pain in my hand spiked. He threw it back hard, right on the numbers as Dad would have said. I fumbled it, but held on to it.

'Yeah, someone has to.' My throw tumbled and bounced on the ground in front of Brent. He picked it up.

'And you wore a dress?' The ball slammed into me again. This time I dropped it and had to run after it.

'A costume." My hand could barely hold the ball, but I chucked it back at Brent.

'You have to snap your wrist,' Brent flipped his wrist like we did when we were making fun of someone for being gay. He threw the ball, softer this time. I tried throwing it back, but the snapping action made my hand worse. The pain drove into my head and I doubled up and puked on the grass.

'Robert!' Mom came running out of the house. She saw the way I held my hand and rounded on Brent. 'What did you do to him?'

'Not his fault,' I said. "I fell in the woods.'

Mom took me to the hospital where they x-rayed my hand, then put a cast on it. When we got home, Brent punched my arm. That was as close to an apology as I was going to get."

"Ophelia?"

Marilyn took a long sip of water.

"Mom decided they should all go and see me perform. I didn't know if any of the other kids' parents were coming, or even if they were allowed. It never came up. We practiced our lines in the clubhouse and no one mentioned the dress. Mack decided they needed costumes too. Joe and Tom almost rebelled when they learned they'd have to wear tights. Mack made them swords too and it was OK. I didn't get a sword; I got flowers. A bunch to hold and some for my hair too.

The day of the performance we trooped down to the gym, where the stage took up one end. Mom and Dad and even Brent sat in chairs along with a few other parents. The class filled up the rest of the chairs. Mack asked if we could go last so we had time to get ready. We watched through scene after scene of bad reading of scenes from Shakespeare's plays. Mack dragged us backstage when the group before us started.

The guys put on their tights with shorts over top of them. Wooden swords stuck awkwardly out of their belts. No one else had costumes. Everyone else had scripts.

Mack handed me the dress.

'Please? Mack never said please. Ever. I put on the dress and he put the flowers in my hair. The others stared at me too. They saw what Mack had seen the first time. I was a different species now. They stood further away. No teasing or joking.

'There's a mirror back here." Tom said. I followed him back to an old mirror.

That wasn't me wearing a dress. The face looking at me wasn't Robert. She had my blue eyes, but the hair wasn't rocker hair. It draped soft and black to the shoulders of the dress. The white daisies looked just right. In the second we stared into each other's eyes she whispered a name to me.

'Come on,' Mack pulled on my shoulder. 'We're on.'

I dragged myself away from the mirror. I don't remember acting out the scene. We must have done OK because everyone applauded. Mr. Telfer talked about how in Shakespeare's time all the actors were men, even the ones who played women's parts. I was the only boy who'd played a girl's part. All the rest had refused. We lined up to take our bows and I looked over to my family. Brent glared at me like he hated me.

We went backstage and took off our costumes. The guys had just downed pants to put on their tights. We'd seen each other in underwear often enough, less than THAT too, but they turned their backs to change back into their pants. I pulled off the dress and took the flowers out of my hair. I didn't want to. Not really, though I don't think I admitted that for ages.

Brent stormed in just after I'd put the dress over the back of a chair. I placed the flowers on top of it. They were just daisies Mack picked in the ditch, but I didn't want to just throw them in the trash.

'What were you doing?' Brent shouted at me. 'How am I supposed to explain that my fucking little brother put on a fucking dress and put fucking flowers in his hair?"

'It's a play,' I said

'No one else did,' Brent punched me in the gut. He'd punched me plenty of times. Brent communicated as much through his violence as his words. I'd been punched on the shoulder in the gut, whatever. This was the first time he meant to hurt me. I bent over and whimpered. He hit me again, and again. I lost count of the blows to my body, my face. Nothing I did could stop him. I had bruises on my arms where I tried to protect myself. My cast cracked. Mr. Telfer and Dad had to pull him off me.

Mom took me to the hospital, by the time we got home, Brent was gone. Dad sent him away to Mom's brother in Nevada. That girl's face in the mirror broke up my family. I hated her at the same time I wanted to be her."

"What was the name she whispered to you?" Dr. Tripp asked.

Marilyn's hands shook as she drank her water. Dr. Tripp looked like he'd wait forever for her to answer the question, so she waited until she thought she could speak without a break in her voice.

"Marilyn" she said, "She told me my name was Marilyn."

"Ah," Dr. Tripp said. "I will see you next week."

Marilyn gathered up her bottle and purse and left without saying goodbye. She couldn't believe after all he'd just tell her *see you next week*. She shook all the way to East Washington Boulevard. Birungi waited at the stop to go to the University.

"You look disarranged. I see you wear my scarf. It looks good on you." Birungi twitched the scarf a little. "I teach you all the ways to use the scarf. You will stun."

Marilyn laughed and the shaking fled.

"Thank you, Birungi, I'd love to learn more about your scarves."

"I wear them because my mother's voice from across the ocean tells me I must. She'd be dead of chagrin if she saw me like this. I tell her I am in America, I don't need to wear scarf. She tells me she is not in America."

Marilyn thought about Brent and Dr. Tripp.

"You can't let other people tell you who you are."

"Not even if I make my mother dead of shame?"

"Do what you decide to do," Marilyn said. "How are we going to help other decide for themselves if we are afraid of our own choices?"

The bus roared up to the stop and they climbed on board. Birungi appeared to be deep in thought, so Marilyn was stuck with her memories. For years, she'd let Brent's absence define who she was. Dr. Tripp probably heard hundreds of these stories. It was his job to listen. Who'd have the time to care about all of them?

"Come to my room," Birungi said when they got off the bus. "I show you my mother and you understand." They walked to the residence and up to her room. It looked like a fabric store exploded in the room, but as Birungi sat and waited quietly the fabric made the room feel like a tent. Even over the window, cloth filtered the light and made it exotic.

"It's beautiful," Marilyn said. "My room is so boring next to this."

"My mother." Birungi handed Marilyn a picture. The woman looked into the camera with a steady stare. Marilyn didn't notice the scarf around the woman's head until she looked for it. She wouldn't want to argue with those eyes.

"Wow," Marilyn said, "she's beautiful, like her daughter."

"She's tall, like you." Birungi grinned. "I'm short like my father." She showed Marilyn another picture. "He died long time back. My mother raised us all. I'm the first to go to University. I win big scholarship; mother not want to shame people by refusing. I say I wear scarf to please mother, but really, I think it is so I do not forget who I am and where I come from. I need to remember if I'm to go back to help them."

"Sounds right to me," Marilyn perched on the bed so she didn't tower over her friend.

"So, you let me teach you about scarf?"

"Sure," Marilyn put her hand up to her neck. then pulled the scarf away and handed it to Birungi. "Teach away."

Birungi showed her the traditional way to wear the scarf. It allowed her to pull it up over her head at a moment's notice. Then she showed Marilyn a dizzying number of other ways to wear it.

"I look on YouTube," Birungi said. "Learn ways of wearing scarf to keep my mother happy, but look like I'm happy to be here.

***

"We talked about self-determination a little last week," Professor Dingman gazed at the class. "and the limits society puts on people's ability to choose. This week we will begin to look at the ways in which we as social workers can increase another person's capacity for good decisions, and ways we can lessen the impact of poor decisions..."

After class Marilyn and Birungi headed to the hall for coffee.

"Look." Anna plunked herself down beside Marilyn. "It isn't like the scarf really hides anything. I know what you are."

"What am I?" Marilyn wished Birungi was here instead of in line for coffee.

"You're a trangender, male to female, but I thought they gave you drugs to stop puberty so..." she waved a hand in front of her throat. "I mean, how did you know?"

"Anna," Marilyn asked, "how do you know you're a girl?"

"I look in the mirror," Anna shrugged a puzzled look on her face. "it's pretty obvious."

"What if it wasn't obvious?" Marilyn asked, "What if the person you saw in the mirror didn't look like the person you felt like? My mirror lies to me every day."

"I don't get it."

"No, you don't." Marilyn snapped her mouth shut on the rest of what she wanted to say.

"So, help me get it," Anna said.

"Why?" Marilyn looked over to where Birungi stood waiting patiently.

"Isn't that what friends do?"

"Birungi treats me the way I see myself," Marilyn said. "We're two girls talking. When you're talking with me, there are two girls, and the boy I used to be. That's one too many people."

"What?" Anna stood up, "I really don't get you."

"No, you don't," Marilyn whispered to Anna's retreating back.

-3-

"Ophelia became my name for the rest of the year," Marilyn said to Dr. Tripp. "Mr. Telfer tried his best, but it was like I was more real as Ophelia than I was as Robert. All the kids in my class called me Ophelia, soon the whole school did. Everyone but the teachers and Mack. I don't know why he called me Robert when even Tom and Joe called me Ophelia."

"You never asked?"

"God, no. I was a twelve year old boy, or I was trying hard to be. I cut my hair the day after the play, but it didn't matter. Every time I saw a mirror, I saw Marilyn looking back. I hated her, so I took up sports. I became like Brent and played everything. Mack wasn't into sports. We drifted apart as I became a jock while he played guitar and wrote songs. We never had a fight, just one day we weren't friends anymore." Marilyn fished in her purse for a tissue. "Shit, my makeup's going to run."

"It's OK." Dr. Tripp handed her a box. "You can fix it before you go."

Marilyn blew her nose and sighed.

"I never thought about it before. I was trying so hard to be Robert, I never saw Mack leaving. One time, I can't remember why, we were sitting in the stands. Something made me ask him about Ophelia. I didn't get past *You remember when I played Ophelia?* He jumped up and ran away. I think he moved soon after, 'cause he wasn't in my class the next year. Tom and Joe were, but they started chasing the girls and I didn't see myself doing that. I wanted as little as possible to do with anything like a girl."

"What about Brent?" Dr. Tripp asked, "Did he call you Robert?"

"He never came home," Marilyn said, "He went to school in Nevada, then joined up in the Marines. Last I heard he'd done a tour in Iraq and had a family down in Texas. We never talked after the play. He vanished. I don't think Mom and Dad knew what to do, and I became enough trouble to keep them from worrying about how to put our family back together."

"So, tell me about the trouble."

"I don't think I was a bully," Marilyn looked at a painting on the wall. "I never hit a kid who didn't want to fight, but I never turned down a fight when one showed up. I found my brother's weights in the garage, so I started lifting weights and doing all the exercises. Even the kids a year ahead of me couldn't stand up to me. Ophelia got shortened to Offie, but there weren't THAT many kids who bothered to talk to me any more. The guys hated me because I could beat them all up if I chose to. The girls hated me because I never cared if they noticed me."

"How did you survive?" Dr. Tripp asked. "It sounds like a very lonely existence."

"I drank, did drugs, played every sport as long as it required me to be tough. That got me through middle school. In High School, I started hearing the rumors."

"Rumors?"

"That I was gay," Marilyn said. "It kind of made sense. I didn't like girls, I started dreaming about the guys I saw in the locker room. That lead to some embarrassing things so I would change off by myself. The only thing keeping me from having the shit kicked out of me was being tougher and meaner than any of them. It meant we won games and they were willing to put up with a lot to win those games."

"So you became the ultimate guy." Dr. Tripp made a note.

"Stupid isn't it?" Marilyn said, "I drove Marilyn down as deep as I could.

The strange thing was the dress. It stayed in my closet all those years. Mack brought it over when I was in the hospital. Dad hung it up in the closet because he didn't know what to do with it. Brent occupied all his time. So when I got home, the dress was hanging in my closet. I pushed it aside, but I never got rid of it."

"The tough guy with a dress in his closet. What did your parents do?"

"They never talked about it. We talked about my behavior, not about who I was. If I didn't tell them different, I was just Robert who'd gone off the rails."

"So what happened then?"

"We're almost done for time," Marilyn said, "and I have to fix my makeup. Can we talk about this next week?"

Dr. Tripp looked at her and tapped his pen on the pad.

"Next week then," he said and a tiny bit of the clenched fist in Marilyn's gut relaxed. She went to the washroom and fixed her makeup. When she stood this close to the mirror, she almost looked like the person she should be.

Marilyn waved to the receptionist and went out to catch her bus.

***

Their social work class talked about the difference between clinical social work and community development.

"Both streams are dedicated to increasing human capacity to live well," Professor Dingman explained, "but the methodologies are very different.

"In clinical social work you interact directly with clients helping them to understand themselves and how they are in the world. It may be through counseling, or in institutional settings. The emphasis is on the change the client needs to experience to move forward. The danger in clinical work is you can get frustrated that client after client needs the same thing. You're on a treadmill and you aren't getting anywhere. The temptation is to short circuit the process and tell the client what they need to do. Giving into that temptation creates greater dependency and lessens rather than increases capacity.

"Community development works with communities and processes rather than individuals. It isn't that people aren't seen as individuals, but rather their importance is what they bring to the table to create larger change in the community. The danger is when change is slow, it is easy to get cynical about the people and processes you work with. The temptation is to go through the motions without any expectation anything will be different. Giving in will make failure inevitable and blaming the people or the system the only way to avoid responsibility."

"What about a person's responsibility to take part in change?" Anna wore a suit and tie and had her blonde hair pulled back tight.

"While everyone has a responsibility to grow." The professor nodded, his signal for what he thought was a good question. "the only growth we really are responsible for is our own."

"So if people don't want to help, we let them off?"

"How can you force them to do anything else? Self-determination includes the possibility the person will make damaging decisions. Actually, damaging decisions are inevitable, and often our task is to help the person recognize the damage and make a plan to repair it."

Marilyn and Blrungi found a table at the Cafe after class.

"I'll get the coffee." Anna dropped what look suspiciously like a briefcase on the table.

Marilyn shrugged and sat down.

"Anna looks different," Birungi looked at Anna in line. "I see pictures of women in suits and they look like women. She tries to look like a man."

"Yeah, I can't wait to hear about this."

Anna came back with the coffee and sat down. She kept fidgeting.

"I hate these pants," she said, "they aren't right."

"So why are you wearing them?" Birungi asked.

"I was thinking about what Marilyn said about how did I know I was a girl. What if I couldn't look in the mirror and see a girl? But I still feel like a girl, just a weird looking girl in a suit." She pulled the tie off and dropped the jacket on the back of the chair. "It was stupid, I know."

"What did you learn?" Marilyn asked.

"I learned I make a really bad guy,"

"Is that all?" Marilyn kept her eyes on her coffee. "I thought I heard you say

THAT you felt like a girl no matter what you looked like."

"I'm a girl," Anna shrugged, "That's all there is to it."

"So am I," Marilyn said.

"But.." Anna stopped and put her head in her hands.

"Your mind is telling me I can't be a girl because I don't look right,"

"You do look different," Anna groaned, "My brain says one thing, you say another."

"Listen to me instead of your brain," Marilyn said. "You don't need to understand it to accept it."

"But I want to understand!" Anna said loud enough people at other tables looked at them. "Shit, now I'm going to die of embarrassment."

"The only way to die of embarrassment is to let it define you." Birungi patted Anna on the arm. "My mother told me growing up is an endless series of embarrassments. Life goes on."

"There is no shame in wanting to understand." Marilyn picked her words carefully. "but you can't expect me to be your object of understanding without being asked."

"Will you help me, please?"

"OK, that's what friends are for." Marilyn grinned at Birungi and patted Anna on the arm.

"Thank you, I'll start by not asking a lot of stupid questions." Anna relaxed her shoulders, and appeared to deliberately shift gears. "Speaking of friends, there's this bar down the street with karaoke every Thursday night."

"Tonight's Thursday," Marilyn said.

"What's karaoke?" Birungi asked.

"It's when you drink enough to get up and sing in front of a room full of strangers," Anna said. "I've always loved singing."

"I've never been big on it," Marilyn said, "but I'll give it a try."

"I can sing," Birungi grinned broadly. "but I don't drink."

"You can come and cheer us on," Anna said. "The sign said they start at eight, so we can meet here at seven thirty?"

***

The Flying Frog looked half pub and half bar. A stage stood at one end of a long room filled with tall tables. On the other half people played pool or laughed in booths. A band played on the stage. They didn't sound bad, but the drummer's timing was off. He switched to playing with one drumstick as he took a slug from a beer bottle. The lead guitarist and singer glanced back and rolled his eyes as if this were a long, losing battle. The woman on keyboards didn't even bother.

"OK," the lead said when the song came crashing to a conclusion. "That's our first set. It's time to break out the karaoke machine and see what damage you can do to the music."

No one rushed forward, so music played from the speakers. The piano player guided the drummer away to a room in the back. The lead guitarist came over to their table.

"Hi, name's Mack. I'm part owner of this place which is the only reason I can get a gig here."

Marilyn expected his eyes to wander to the other girls then come back to her as he tried to make her fit the concept in his head. He barely looked at them, instead he stared at Marilyn as if she held the answer to a deep question.

"What did you think of the music?"

Marilyn saw her friends trying to come up with something polite.

"You're pretty good," she said, "but your drummer is off and dragging you down."

"You a musician?" Mack asked, "You know what he's been through?"

"Long, long time ago, I played drums." She shrugged slightly. "I know a little about the things that drive people to drink. "

"Right," Mack said, "don't be shy. Let me know what you want to sing."

They sipped their drinks while a couple of girls sang a duet, then a man sang a song that soared painfully out of his range. Anna went up and sang surprisingly well.

"Come on, Marilyn," she said, "It's your turn."

Birungi nodded.

Marilyn sighed and took a sip of her Caesar.

"Ok." She got up and went over to where Mack had the computer running the karaoke.

"Do you have something that doesn't go too high?"

"You know *Feeling Good?*"

"Sure, doesn't everyone?"

He cued up the music and the words. Marilyn stood at the mike and looked out at the bar. She could barely see Anna and Birungi giving her the thumbs up. The words came up, and she started singing. She was a little surprised she could. The words and the music carried her away to someplace where she didn't always have to explain herself, where she was just Marilyn with no strange looks or awkward questions and it did feel good.

The applause when she finished made her blush and Anna hugged her as she sat down.

"Let's do a duet next."

"Do they have trios?" Birungi asked.

Mack found them an Andrews Sister piece none of them knew, but they laughed and giggled their way through it. There were only a couple of people Marilyn had ever had so much fun with. She went up to sing solo again and did another jazz number.

"Hey," Mack said, "a round of applause for our newest diva. Now I'm back up with my group to show you just how good she was singing."

The keyboardist came out and shook her head slightly. Mack frowned and looked at Marilyn.

"If your drum playing is half as good as your singing..."

"Oh no," Marilyn put up her hands, but Anna and Birungi pushed her toward the stage.

Marilyn sat herself behind the drums and picked up the drumsticks. She'd never used real drumsticks, the nerves she expected to feel before she sang hit her full force.

"Just keep the beat," Mack said back to her, then counted in the song. Marilyn got the timing in her head and tapped it out on the drum. The first song she just tapped the beat. In the second, she started using the foot pedal. The cobbled together set from years ago, she'd kick the tub she had as a base drum. In the third piece, she started trying some riffs and additions. She watched Mack as he played. It was just like days in the clubhouse before Ophelia. The fourth song was an original and Marilyn almost lost the rhythm of the music. She knew this song, or more truthfully, she knew its ancestor. They'd been practicing it the week before Mr. Telfer handed out scripts and Robert died.

Marilyn forced herself to play as waves of ice and fire rolled through her veins. What if he recognized her? What if he didn't?

"A round of applause for our guest drummer!" Mack announced at the end of the song. "You Ok?" he whispered, "Cher gave me the trouble sign."

"I'm good," she said before miraculously walking to her table without falling over or getting sick.

"Water," she replied to the server when he came to ask her what she wanted to drink.

The water flowed down her throat and she imagined it cooling the heat, easing the ice. Whatever happened, she'd be all right.

They finished the set then Mack and Cher came over to her table.

"Thanks for filling in," Mack said.

"You were great," Cher said, "I can't believe Mack didn't warn you about the original."

"That's fine," Marilyn said, "I knew it from years ago."

Mack stared at her for a long time, then he mouthed *Robert,* but what he said was "Ophelia?"

"I'm Marilyn now." She threw her arms around him. "I was thinking about you just the other day, and now here you are."

"Careful, you'll make Cher jealous." But he wrapped her just as tight and held her a long time.

"I'm guessing you're from one of his old groups," Cher raised an eyebrow.

"Smells like Rock and Roll," Marilyn said.

"I thought that was all guys." Cher wrinkled her forehead.

"It was," Mack said.

"I was Robert back then." Marilyn surprised herself at how easy it was to say.

"I should have known from the voice." Cher nodded and patted Marilyn on the shoulder. "But I got distracted by the talent. I've got to go check on Bo. You guys get caught up."

"Bo is our drummer, when he hasn't drunk himself into a stupor." Mack sighed.

"Why keep him on then?" Anna asked.

"Because he's a damn good drummer when he's sober. He usually makes it through the second set. I'd love to talk, but I have things to take care of as the manager of this place. Can you come by at lunch tomorrow and I'll introduce you to the crew."

"Sure," Marilyn said, "That would be great."

-4-

"So, I went to the Flying Frog at lunch, and Mack and I got caught up. He's been putting together groups and playing music all these years. He met Cher in high school and they got married right after graduation. They had a group all ready to hit the bar scene when Cher's dad died and left them half the Flying Frog. Mack said it was a choice of staying home and working for a living or going on tour. When Cher told him she was pregnant, that was it. They stayed put and he and Cher have a house band on weeknights and they bring in acts on weekends. I met Crista, their little girl and she's so cute. She has her own little guitar."

"Marilyn," Dr. Tripp looked at her. "We'll come back to your friends in a while, but there's some work we need to do."

"Why? Why do I need to go through all this? I know what I want."

"True," Dr. Tripp said, "but do you know who you are?"

"That doesn't make sense."

"When it does, we'll be close to finished." Dr. Tripp picked up the pad and pen. "You told me Robert went off the rails. Let's start there."

"Fine," Marilyn slouched in the seat. "People thought I was gay. I didn't care if they left me along. Sports made me important and booze and drugs numbed me. I didn't need anything else. Not until I got this huge crush on a guy on the football team. I'd looked at gay porn on the computer. Why not if I was gay? It didn't do anything for me. When I had dreams about him, it wasn't me he was with. That bitch Marilyn was there doing all the things I wanted to, but she had the right parts. I had to hide in the locker room because my body didn't know the difference. So, I hit the booze and shit harder. The coach busted me and threw me off the team.

"Suddenly, I didn't matter. I had nobody. I was nobody.

"At home thinking I'd break into my Dad's liquor and get pissed, I broke the hinges with a crowbar and stole the oldest bottle of scotch there. Mom was at work and so was Dad. I sat in my room and killed most of a half bottle of twenty-five-year-old scotch, until I could barely stand. I can't remember getting undressed or putting the dress on. Sometimes the dress would move from the back of the closet to the front, like I'd been wearing it, though I couldn't ever recall it. This time I remember looking in the mirror. Marilyn was there. She was crying and shaking her head; like Mom when I'd been caught doing another stupid thing. Then she walked away and left me looking at myself. All I could see was a fucked-up bastard wearing a stupid white dress.

"All that time I'd been hating Marilyn, I'd been killing myself. I smashed the mirror with the bottle. It broke in my hand and cut me deep. I sat on the floor and stared at the blood. Only thing was, it didn't hurt. I knew it had to hurt. That's when I cut my wrists with the glass. Then it hurt, it hurt so much. But I deserved it 'cause I killed Marilyn. I tried to cut deeper, but I couldn't hold the bottle any more. I howled, I guess. The police said that's why our neighbor called them; she was scared of the noise. They came in and saw me. The ambulance took me away to the hospital where they sewed up the cuts and filled me with drugs and put me in a psych ward.

"Mom came and cried. Dad didn't come, Mom told me it was too hard on him. I wandered through the ward drugged up to my eyeballs. After a while the psychiatrist decided on a proper medication for me and sent me home.

The meds worked. They put a wall between me and reality. Life was fucked up, but I couldn't feel it. Mom bought me this guitar and a book about how to play it. I never learned any songs, but I'd play chords for hours just zoning out.

"I went back to school with these big ugly scars and looked stoned all the time. Mom thought I should try something completely different, so she convinced the music teacher to let me play in Jazz Band. All those hours of playing chords meant I had fingers like leather. I played the chords on the music and starting enjoying myself. Music became my new drug of choice. The psychiatrist let me cut back on the dosage of the pills and the fog lifted. It was my last chance to be a normal guy, so I didn't stop Marlene when she started hitting on me.

"We went out to movies and to dances. I liked her and we had lots of fun, but we never did anything. I couldn't even kiss her good night. We were just friends and I couldn't explain why. She thought it was the medication I was on. We decided I'd stop taking it. I'd taken it so long without a problem it was easy to fool Mom. The fog vanished, and I felt like a complete person again. There wasn't anything between me and the world. Marlene and I went to a dance, but we cut out early and went back to my house. My Mom and Dad had gone to friends for the evening.

We put some slow music on and danced. I like dancing, but when she started feeling me up, nothing happened. She made me put my hands on her and still nothing happened. She even took her dress off and kissed me. I didn't want to be kissing her.

'What is wrong with you?' she said to me. 'Don't you want me? Are you gay after all?'

'I'm not a lesbian,' I told her.

'You can't be a lesbian, you're not a girl.'

'Yes, I am.'

'What are you talking about?'.

'I'm a girl,' I said, 'really.'

'You're nuts,' She put her dress back on and left. She never talked to me again.

I sat and stared into space for the longest time. Then it was like Marilyn came and sat down inside me.

It's time she told me.

Yeah, I know. That's when Robert finally left. He just faded away like a ghost and I was Marilyn,

"Very good," Dr. Tripp said, "but that's our time for today. I'd like to hear more about you becoming Marilyn next week."

"I told you I am Marilyn."

He laughed, and Marilyn tensed up.

"Nobody just is, Marilyn," he said, "we spend our whole live becoming."

"Becoming what?"

"Who we are."

"That doesn't make any sense." Marilyn packed her purse and stood up.

"The most important things often don't." Dr. Tripp looked down at his notes.

Marilyn shook her head and left to catch the bus.

A poster on the bus shelter caught her eye.

'So Sing Already', a new live talent show. If you think you can sing, come out and audition. First prize is a record deal and a national tour.

Marilyn turned away from the poster to board her bus as it pulled up. *As if, I don't need that hassle.*

***

"It is important to have clear goals and objectives." Professor Dingman wrote the words on the board. "Goals are longer term and have a broader sweep. *Making the world a better place by healing one person at a time.* is a goal. It doesn't have any time limits, it's hard to measure if you've achieved it, but the process is clear. By healing people, we make the world a better place.

"An objective might be *to provide quality mental health care to the people of North Seattle by opening a low-cost clinic.* This is measurable, we know how many people use the clinic, we may also be able to learn our effectiveness by interviewing past clients of the service. It is local; we are putting this clinic in North Seattle, and we know who our clientele is."

"Excuse me," a secretary stuck her head in the door of the room. "Is Marilyn Johnson here? I have a message that she is to phone home. It's urgent."

Marilyn scrambled out of her seat and followed the secretary. She didn't notice Birungi and Anna following her until they got to the door.

"Look, we'll wait out here," Anna said, "but if it's bad enough to pull her out of class, she needs some friends."

The secretary shrugged and showed Marilyn where she could make the call from.

"Hi, Mom," Marilyn said, "what's going on?"

"I want you to know he's going to be OK, but your Dad had a heart attack."

"But he's OK?"

"Yes, he's in the hospital, but the doctors say he'll be fine." Her mother stopped talking and Marilyn wondered what news was worse than her father's heart attack.

"He got laid off when things got slow," her mom said, "the insurance is saying we didn't pay the premiums. We thought his company was paying them, but they didn't. We've talked to other people and they're in the same boat, but lawyers move slow and courts slower.

In the meantime, we've had to sell off everything we could to pay the bills."

"Use my University money," Marilyn said, "I'll get a job and figure something out."

"That's just it," her mom said, "we already used it. We're going to have to sell the house and move down with Brent if they'll let us. We need your special fund."

"It's OK, Mom." Marilyn tried not to scream into the phone, "Taking care of Dad is more important than whether I have a penis or not." She tried to ignore the shocked look on the secretary's face.

"I'm sorry, dear." Her mom sounded like she was fighting tears. "I know what this means to you."

"It will be OK." Marilyn tried to believe it and make it true. She'd been looking forward to the surgery and finally having something like the body she knew she should have.

"Brent's calling," her mom said, "I'll talk to you later." She hung up and Marilyn stood listening to the dial tone. The secretary took the phone from her hand as her friends took her arms and sat her down. Someone handed her a glass of water and Marilyn gulped it back.

"I hate calls like this," the secretary said, "I'm Ms. Chisolm."

Marilyn looked at her. She wore a loose blouse and pants THAT did little to hide her size, but her brown eyes glistened with tears. "Now I want you to know your fees are paid to the end of the term. So is your housing, so you don't have to stop classes and live on the street. There is a student employment center if you need to look for a job. If you have a problem, any problem, you come and see me and I'll try to help you figure it out."

"Thanks," Marilyn said, "I will."

"So?" Anna asked when they were out in the hall, "what is going on? You looked like someone died."

"Not quite," Marilyn said, "my dad had a heart attack. He's going to be OK, but—"

"That is good, right?" Birungi put her hand on Marilyn's arm. "Your doctors will make him strong again."

"Yes, "but the insurance company says they aren't covered."

"Oh no," Anna gasped and covered her mouth. "what about your university?"

"Gone," Marilyn moaned, "all of it gone."

"But you have until December to find a job and make some money to pay for your tuition. You can come live in my room." Anna counted on her fingers, "We'll get you to Student Services and they'll help with a resume and... Shit! This isn't fair, you'd be a great social worker. Maybe there are some scholarships you can apply for. I'll go back and ask." She headed back to the office while Birungi led Marilyn to the hall. She didn't have to wait in line for the coffee so she was sitting down with Marilyn when the students from the class mobbed around her and demanded to know what had happened.

"Here are some forms." Anna appeared at her side. "Don't worry about them now, I'll help you with them later. The due date is next week. They said there's no guarantee. With interest rates low, there isn't a lot of money."

Birungi sat and drank coffee. She didn't say a word, but her hand never left Marilyn's

They dragged Marilyn to the Flying Frog for karaoke. Marilyn only drank water. The smallest loss of inhibition might send her over into the abyss. She only sang a couple of songs and shook her head when Mack asked if she'd play drums for the second set.

"Something's wrong," Mack sat down across from her. "You can tell me, or I'll give them free booze until they tell me."

"My dad had a heart attack." Marilyn marveled she could now say those words without feeling like she'd shatter into a million pieces. She explained about the money.

"Well, I can do something for you," Mack said. "One of my servers quit, they're always quitting. You can work evenings so the tips are better. You can even sing karaoke Thursday night and help with the band. Start as soon as you think you're ready."

"Shouldn't you check with Cher first?"

"She won't mind, really. Come by for lunch again and we'll sort out the details."

***

"Do you have any serving experience?" Cher looked at Marilyn, "You'll need to watch when it gets crowded. It does get crowded some weekends. The big thing is to get the drinks right then get them quickly. It does no one any good if you rush and get the wrong order. If you need to write it down at first, do THAT. Don't apologize or the guys will try to take advantage of you. They will try to take advantage of you anyway, but if you keep it professional you have half a chance."

Bo wandered out of the back room.

"You're the one who's been playing my drums."

"That's right,"

"At least you didn't move them around, you got some sense." He put a couple of sticks down on the table in front of her. "Let's hear you."

Marilyn walked over and sat down behind the drums.

"Well," Bo said, "play."

"There's no music."

"Play to the music in your head," Bo sounded like he was ready to give up on her. Marilyn closed her eyes and started playing. Bo came over and corrected the way she held the drumsticks. She started again, but he waved her silent.

"Put some music behind her."

Mack picked up his guitar and Cher sat at the piano.

"Just keep the beat," Mack said and counted her in. Bo muttered and complained through the entire three songs they played before Marilyn stood up.

"You show me how it's done." She held out the drumsticks.

Bo sat at the drums and gave a four beat. He played around the music, when Mack lagged a little Bo pushed him back to the pace, when Cher ran ahead he pulled her back.

"How do I learn to play like that?" Marilyn asked.

"If she can hear it, she can play it," Mack said.

"Your kid can play better drums." Bo shook his head.

"Not if you teach her." Mack stuck out his lip stubbornly.

"What do you think, Cher?" Bo asked.

"Don't ask me. I'm just the hired help."

Mack opened his mouth to argue, but Cher crossed her arms and glared at him.

"Your call, Bo," Mack said. "She'll serve the early set, but we're losing people in the second set."

"You. Be here every day." Bo pointed his finger at Marilyn. "Listen to music all the time. Sleep with music in your ears, shower, walk, eat with the music playing, hell fuck with the music in your head. If you don't hear the music, you can't play." He got up and walked into the back room.

Crista picked up Bo's sticks and banged on the drums. Bo was right. The kid played better than she did.

-5-

"I'm sorry to hear of your financial difficulties," Dr. Tripp put his pad down. "Unfortunately, my bookkeepers don't let me do pro bono work, so unless you can pay for the sessions, this will be our last one. Whatever they say, this one's on me."

"We're almost done anyway," Marilyn said.

"Actually, we're just getting started," Dr. Tripp leaned forward in his chair. "but finish telling me how you got here."

"After Marlene left, I sat in the dark for hours until Mom and Dad got home.

'Robert,' Mom said, 'What are you doing sitting in the dark?'

'I'm not Robert, I'm Marilyn.'

'What are you talking about?' Dad asked.

'Remember when you watched me play Ophelia? That was me, not this." I waved my hands at my body.

'What, you're telling me you're a girl?'

'That's right,' I started shaking, 'I been fighting it for so long trying to be the boy you wanted me to be, but I can't do it any longer.'

'I don't understand," Dad unlocked the cabinet and poured himself a drink. 'I don't understand.' I shook more and more. Mom gasped for air behind me. Dad sat down beside me and put his arm around my shoulders. 'Why didn't you talk to me?' I barely took in the words, he spoke so softly, but warmth starting moving from the knot in my gut. Tears poured from my eyes as my Dad pulled me tight. All those years I thought my Dad was like Brent.

'I'll call the hospital,' Mom's voice so flat and dead my heart shattered.

'No,' Dad said, 'not until we find someone who can help Marilyn, not just drug her.'

"They talked all night. I fell asleep on the couch while my parents argued over who I was. Mom shook my shoulder to wake me up.

'Marilyn, time for breakfast.'

"All that time I was afraid of what my parents would think, and they changed everything they knew about me overnight. Never once have they ever slipped up and called me Robert or referred to me as *he.* I don't know what it cost them. Mom always seemed hesitant around me. Dad reminded me every day I could talk to him."

"I wish all my patients had parents as brave as yours." Dr. Tripp smiled at her.

"Yeah, I heard some stories," Marilyn said, "Dad found me a group, and I learned my life was a walk in the park compared to some. I started dressing as girl, mostly. Dad went to bat with the School Board and got me transferred into a different high school. He hoped a fresh start would be easier than changing in my old surroundings."

"Yes, and no," Dr. Tripp said.

"So I found out. Some of the problem, I created myself. The principal heard of me from the other school. The Board didn't let me register as a girl. I had to register as a trans and have my own bathroom. I was angry, so I grew a beard and deliberately flouted my masculine body and feminine personality. As you can imagine, I didn't make many friends. Only there was one girl, Tuni, the first person to just see me as myself without needing to draw boxes around me. She almost made me want to be a boy, just so I could be with her. She figured out it wouldn't work and we were fantastic friends for the rest of the term."

"What happened to her?" Dr. Tripp asked. "That it was only one term?"

"She almost died because of me. Tuni didn't want to stay around the school after that. She just wrote all the exams, graduated early and left on an internship with some magazine. I think she's in India researching changing attitudes toward women."

"She sounds extraordinary."

"Yeah," Marilyn said, "it's impossible to keep up with her."

"So, how did the second term go?"

"Compared to the first one, it went smooth as silk. I shaved the beard and lost the attitude. Tuni put herself on the line for me, I couldn't do any less than live up to her. I met a guy named John Wayne. He was Korean and his parents were western fans. He was gay and had a thing for me. The only problem was what he loved about me were the things I wanted to change. It was fun while it lasted and we're still friends. He's playing football down east."

"And now you are here," Dr. Tripp said, "and ready to begin the journey."

"With the money gone, I can't afford the surgery."

"There are groups who do the surgery for free." Dr. Tripp stood. "As you might imagine, there is a considerable waiting list, but it is worth investigating. My receptionist will give you some information. While you wait, you may want to continue thinking about the difference between who you are, and what your body is. Good luck, Marilyn."

To her shock, she broke down in tears as soon as she left the office. The receptionist gave her tissues and a fat envelope full of information and forms.

She wandered out into the sun to wait for her bus. The poster on the shelter caught her eye. This time she pulled it down and stuffed it into her purse.

***

"It is important not to confuse our expectations with our goals and objectives." Professor Dingman never asked about the phone call. He didn't treat her any differently. Certainly, the marks on the papers she handed in didn't show any preferential treatment. Whatever else she had to do, Marilyn needed this credit to continue her education. The other two courses were simple. Professor Dingman demanded they think. Tuni would love this course.

"Our expectations are what we project out into the world in order to make sense of it. If we tried to exist with no expectations at all we'd be overwhelmed as we constantly needed to remake decisions we'd made the day before. Imagine if you had to decide each day which of the many assorted varieties of coffee you would drink because you never knew what you wanted."

"Sounds like Cameron," someone called from the back. Cameron grinned and shrugged.

"Guilty as charged, though I should state I have an objective of trying each kind by the end of the term."

"And what of your expectations?" the professor asked.

"Meh," Cameron said, "some are good and some not so good."

"So your expectation is you will enjoy each variety equally."

"I guess so."

"What if you had stated an objective of liking each kind of coffee by the end of the term?"

"But I can't predict what I'll like and what I won't."

"Exactly." The professor beamed at Cameron as if he'd said something brilliant. Cameron looked confused.

"Expectations are necessary," the professor said, "but they are inevitable doomed to failure. We can't control the things necessary to fulfill our expectations."

"So if I expect people to treat me with respect regardless of my skin colour, it won't happen?" Cameron asked.

"Not all the time, eventually you will meet up with an incorrigible racist, or a good person on a bad day. This is why is it important to be aware of our expectations and keep them separate from our objectives."

"So I could have an objective to reduce racism through community awareness, but be wary of my expectation of being treated with respect."

"Correct again," Professor Dingman said.

"So, if we are paying attention to our expectations, we won't use them to wrongly evaluate the effectiveness of our objectives?" Anna asked.

"The Cafe must be putting out a high grade of caffeine today." The professor grinned. "But all good things must come to an end. Class is dismissed, may I remind you, I expect the next paper to be in on Monday? Midterms begin soon, if you have any questions check my office hours on the syllabus. It is easier to solve your problems before they become poor grades."

Marilyn didn't have time to linger over coffee with Anna and Birungi. Bo expected her to be at the bar soon for another session of brow beating. She tapped her fingers on her legs as she walked, trying to get the riff Bo taught her into her head. No, into her hands, he kept telling her to play with her hands so she could think about the music instead of worrying about the drums.

"Hi Crysta." Marilyn waved as she entered. "Is Uncle Bo up?"

Crysta shook her head and played on her guitar. Marilyn sat at the drums and starting playing. The rhythm was wrong for what Crysta was doing and she stuck her tongue out at Marilyn. Marilyn adjusted her playing until Crysta laughed and danced around the stage.

"That's enough, Crysta," Cher poked her head through the door. "Time to get you to Sarah's."

Crysta put the tiny guitar down and ran out the door with her mom.

"You almost sounded good," Bo came out of the room where he lived. Marilyn never saw inside of it and had no desire to.

"What's her problem?" Marilyn asked.

"Crysta's four. Her fingers don't move so fast yet."

"No, I mean Cher."

"Oh, what did you expect after walking in here, singing better than she dreamed of, and being a walking, talking fascination for her husband? She used to be the one Mack asked to fill gaps in when the karaoke got slow. Now it's all you babe."

"I thought she liked me."

"Where did you get that idea? Mack likes you. He probably wishes he'd stuck around for the big transformation. For

Cher, you're competition, and probably trouble. Her dad was in the business. She knows the pain he put her mother through. I was the cause of half of it, but Cher tolerates me because I'm not going to run off with her man. He's not my type. You aren't either, but give me a call when you get your new plumbing and I'll test drive it for you.'

"Fuck you."

"That's the general idea" Bo leered at her. "Now let's hear that riff."

Marilyn wanted to walk out, but she needed the job and she needed Mack. It wasn't that she wanted to sleep with him, but he gave her a constant quiet reassurance she craved like a drug. When she was around him, she had no doubt in her abilities.

Bo ran her over the riff until she hated it.

"You're playing with your head," he said. "You need to practice until you can play it in your sleep. When you get into the zone it's like you have all these possibilities and nothing is real until you make it real. There is nothing else like it."

"If it's so glorious, why do you drink until you can't play?" She went to the table to get her water and grab a head ache pill from her purse.

"The only thing keeping me from drinking is drumming and sex. I'm not doing so good on either of those, am I?" He shoved his hands in front of her. They shook almost uncontrollably. "I don't shake because I drink; I drink because I shake. If I drink just the right amount the shaking stops, but I can't stop there. The booze pulls me in until I can't play at all. The only reason I'm not dead is 'cause I owe Cher's old man. If you think you're going fuck with her, you'll have to go through me. Don't you tell her anything either. I won't have her pitying me."

"Damn," Marilyn dug through her purse. The idea of pitying Bo made her headache worse. She dumped everything on the table and grabbed the bottle. She threw a couple of pills in her mouth and drank more water.

"What's this?" Bo held up the poster from the talent show.

"Contest I'm thinking of entering."

"Bah. contests are ruining the business." Bo frowned. "Nobody wants to work at it. They want to go on a show, sing a song, tell a sob story, get famous. The real talent isn't the ability to play. There's thousands of people who can play. The real talent is being persistent enough so you can grab opportunity by the tits when she walks by."

"This isn't an opportunity?"

"This is a gong show." Bo waved the poster. "You win. Then what? How are you going to know how to work your heart out if you never had to do it before? Singing brilliantly once on TV is easy, singing every day so people don't walk out on you is hard."

"What about Mack?"

"Mack's got a family, what does he need with fame?"

He pointed back to the drum set. Marilyn swept everything back into her purse and stuffed the poster in too. Then she walked over to the drums and started working them again.

Her headache didn't ease up all night, but Marilyn smiled at customers and served drinks. She stayed in the shadows. The tips weren't as good and the harassment worse, but the people couldn't see her well. When she sang, she threw Birungi's scarf around her neck. No one could see her back on the drums.

"Cher," Marilyn said after close, "do you have a second?"

"We can't afford to give you a raise." Cher didn't look up from the cash. "We're barely making the nut as it is."

"I don't want a raise. I want to tell you I'm not after Mack."

"Get out." Cher pointed at the door. "Don't come back."

"Shit," Marilyn put her hand against her head. "I can't think." Tears leaked down her face, burning tracks into her cheeks.

"Give the girl a break," Bo set himself down at the table.

"I didn't know you were out here."

"Can hardly teach the girl if I don't listen to her." He kept his hand on his knees beneath the table. "You should know she's been working wounded. She had a headache this afternoon and from the looks of her it hasn't left."

"Ok, say your piece." Cher sighed deeply. "Before Mack comes and makes it a complete circus."

"I don't want Mack. I wouldn't know what do with him if I had him. What I want is this job without worrying I'm busting up my friends' marriage. I'm not good at this." Marilyn massaged her head. To her surprise, Cher walked behind her and began rubbing her head.

"Keep talking. I'm not convinced."

"You get rid of Marilyn," Bo said, "Mack won't think you trust him. It isn't far from not feeling trusted to not being trustworthy."

"You would know."

"I do, girl; to my everlasting regret."

"So, what do you want me to do?"

"Tell me if things are getting out of hand," Marilyn said, "and I'll quit."

"You should quit now," Yet Cher's hands didn't stop, "but Bo's right, and the bastard knows it. If Mack starts confessing to you, it's time to quit. I'll be sorry to lose you, but I'd rather have Mack than you. You," Cher glared at Bo, "don't think I don't see those hands shaking. You do what you have to." She rested her hands on Marilyn's shoulders with her fingers lightly touching her throat. "If you breathe a word of this to

Mack, I'll fire you, then rehire you so I can kick your ass and fire you again. Now get on home before the headache comes back."

Marilyn stood up and overbalanced for a second as she realized the pain was gone.

"I only seen her work that magic on two people, and neither was me." Bo put his hands in his pockets and walked back to his room.

-6-

"I don't get this thing about expectations being separate from our objectives." Marilyn sat in Professor Dingman's office and tried not to beg. Her marks in this course weren't good, and it was a prerequisite for most of the courses in her degree.

"Describe a situation where your expectations weren't met."

"I'm learning to play the drums," Marilyn pushed aside her discomfort. "It's sort of part of my job. Bo, the guy teaching me is the meanest, crudest person I've met."

"Are you learning to play the drums?"

"I just told you I was."

"Let me rephrase the question. Are you getting better at the drums?"

"I think so."

"Then his teaching methods may be unorthodox, but they are effective."

"But shouldn't he treat me with more respect?"

"Why? As horrible as he sounds, he's teaching you and you are learning. If he changed his methods, would you learn as well? Maybe, maybe not. I would hazard a guess if he starts being pleasant and helpful, he will stop being a good instructor."

Marilyn's heart sank as the conversation from the night before replayed in her head.

"You are not the first transgendered student to come through my class and I sincerely hope you won't be the last. As a transgendered person, you expect people to be conscious of how they use gender and where they place you in the web of gender as compared to where you place yourself. This awareness takes a great deal of effort, so most people avoid it by pretending the need doesn't exist. They either ignore you or assign an arbitrary gender and stay with it regardless of what you say." He lifted an eyebrow at Marilyn and she nodded.

"Now your objective is to learn to play the drums." The eyebrow went up again.

"Yes, but..." something began to take shape in her mind. "I'm getting in the way, because I'm expecting him to treat me like everyone else does. I could just focus on the learning and leave the rest. I've been through worse." She shook her head,

"So I have to do this for everything?"

"No," the professor said, "just the times when your expectations get in the way of your objective. It won't always be as easy as this example, but the more you watch for it, the easier it becomes to spot. On the other hand, it is one reason why all social workers are supervised. Given that we work so much in the field of emotions and feelings it behooves us to be very aware of our own."

"Thank you, Professor Dingman," Marilyn went to her room to think and work on her readings. Between classes and working part time she didn't have a lot of time to study.

A knock at her door interrupted her work. Marilyn thought she was just beginning to put the pieces together.

"Yes?"She yanked the door open. She caught a glimpse of Birungi's face falling before Anna stepped forward.

"You're neglecting your friends." She poked Marilyn in the shoulder. "I know you work and you have courses, but your social life is important too. We are, after all, studying to be social workers."

Marilyn caught a glimpse of something before it vanished. Something about what the professor explained to her.

"You're right," Marilyn put school work out of her mind. "I have the night off, so I am at your disposal."

Birungi smiled again and Anna grabbed her arm.

"Quick, before she comes to her senses and changes her mind." They hauled her away laughing and giggling.

"Tonight is a good night." Birungi squeezed Marilyn's hand. "We have a surprise for you."

"Don't give her all the details," Anna waggled her finger. "We must soften her up."

Softening her up included taking her out for a hamburger across the street from the University.

"It is rumored, they use real meat here." Anna looked at her burger.

"What is the university supposed to use?" Birungi asked.

"I don't know, but I've heard it comes from the Chem labs." Marilyn laughed at Birungi's face then took a huge bite of her burger.

To her shock, her friends dragged back into the university toward the campus pub. They usually avoided it as being too full of desperate first year nerds trying to pick up girls. A big poster in the window advertised *Talent Night.*

"In light of a certain TV show coming here to recruit talent, we decided we should get our dibs in first. Now is your chance at fame,"

"or humiliation,"

"or maybe both."

The judges looked to be senior students paid in beer for their judging efforts. They made no effort to be fair or impartial; praising good looking girls and trashing the men regardless of the perceived talent.

"Go on," Anna said, "It will be fun."

"Remind me again why I let you talk me into this," Marilyn cringed as the trio insulted a big woman with a somewhat shrill operatic style voice.

"Maybe they will be surprised when someone can really sing," Birungi said.

"I heard that." The closest judge beckoned imperiously. "Come forward and be judged!"

Marilyn walked out onto the stage.

"It's a valkyrie," one judge said.

"Don't be silly," another one replied, "What's the feminine of valkyrie?"

"It's already feminine," Marilyn grinned.

"Ah, like moose then," the first judge said.

"What are you going to sing," the student at the computer asked. Marilyn pointed to a title on his screen. The student shrugged. "It's your funeral."

The music came up.

"What this? Old blue eyes?" The judge covered his eyes. "We're not worthy."

Marilyn laughed and launched into *My Way*. The judges looked like the three monkeys with one's hands over his eyes, one's on his ears and one's over his mouth. But the first was peeking through his fingers, the second had his hands cupped to hear better, while the third was covering up laughter. She let the song take her where it wanted while she played it up to the delight of the audience.

The song finished, and the judges broke into applause and made a show of standing up.

"At last," one shouted, "an act we can listen to,"

"and watch,"

"and not puke,"

"We dub thee the grand prize winner."

The grand prize turned out to be a university t-shirt with *We Gots Talent* scribbled on it.

"Sorry, left over from last year's show." the judge whispered. The hundred dollars cash was going to be more useful.

"It's traditional to buy the judges a round."

"or three."

Marilyn put the bills away inside her shirt and went back to her friends.

"Quite an act," a man said. He looked too old to be the usual university crowd. "Carl Sminck" he introduced himself, "I'm with the actual show," he gave her a card.

"So you're going to offer her a private audition?" Anna snatching the card from Marilyn.

"That would be very inappropriate, and a waste of time," Carl said, "since I'm neither a judge nor heterosexual. Just show for the audition. If you want a word of advice, the judges are suckers for a good sob story. If they buy it, the audience buys it. Your voice is decent, it will likely get you to the live show, a good story will get you to the final. Good night ladies." He walked away through the crowd.

"You should so audition for this," Anna gave her the card back.

"He did say you sang well," Birungi beamed a smile at Marilyn.

"What he said was I sang decently, but if I played the judges I could make the finals."

"Did you not play the judges here?"

"This is different. This is just a night out with good friends. It didn't matter if I won. With this," she waved the card, "everything would change."

"It's going to change anyway," Anna said. "Why not for the good?"

"But I just got things the way I want them," Marilyn moaned.

"That's life," Anna shrugged. "Think about it, Ok?"

"He said I needed a good sob story." Marilyn put her hand on Anna's arm. "That's on you guys."

***

"Slimy bastards are everywhere," Bo tossed the card back at her. "They need cannon fodder for their show. He's out drumming up talent to fill the place and make it look real, for all you know the fix is already in. He's right though, you need a real good story to get anywhere. You can't make it up though, they'll eat you alive on the web. You'd be horrified at what they can find out about you out there."

"So, I'm a transgendered person whose dad had a heart attack and used up all my university money."

Bo rolled his eyes.

"And surgery money,"

"It's a family show, babe."

"My parents moved in with my brother who tried to kill me when I was a kid when I first came out as a girl. I haven't talked to him in seven years."

Bo nodded his head.

"You're going in the right direction."

"My brother is a serving Marine?"

"You'd best not mention the killing part," Bo said, "his superiors might not like it."

"How about if I dedicate the song to him?"

"Killer stuff, kid, there won't be a dry eye in the house. You have to work it hard. Like the drumming, so you don't have to think about the words, just what they're doing to the judges' cold, little hearts." Bo sighed and sat at the table. "Take it from an old man, Marilyn, you won't like what they make you into. You're better to stay here, get your degree and make a real fucking difference in the world."

"I'm going to finish my degree, no matter what."

"Really?"

"Absolutely,"

"Even when you're on tour?"

"They have correspondence courses, Bo. I'll keep up."

"What if they offer to put you under the knife tomorrow in exchange for your soul?"

Marilyn opened her mouth, but no words came out.

"That's what I thought, kid. Just pray they don't learn your price." He walked back into his room. Marilyn stared at the closed door, then sat in the stool and worked the riffs until her arms ached.

***

The Frog was packed, and Marilyn kept busy picking up unusually big tips and fending off more than usual groping hands. It was a relief when Mack asked her up to sing. Until the crowd started cheering and chanting her name. She sang three songs, and didn't think anybody heard a word of them. They quieted a little for Mack's set. Marilyn played the entire set. She felt safer behind the drums. Bo had to help push the crowd out the door. Cher rushed off to pick up Crysta from their sitter.

Mack came and sat down beside her.

"Quite a night,"

"Sorry about that," Marilyn said.

Mack laughed.

"Sorry? We probably made our nut for the week just tonight. That means the weekend's ours. A few more nights like this and we might finally get ahead."

"That would be good."

"You know, the first time you put on that dress, I fell for you." Mack said.

Marilyn's heart pounded. *No, not now you fool.* But he couldn't read her mind, and she couldn't think of the words to say.

"That song we sing in the second set? *Don't you have a sister?*"

"Humming a few harmonies hardly means I'm singing it." Marilyn wanted to get up and run. Her legs wouldn't move, her arms barely held her weight as she leaned on them. Why did it have to be on this stage? It was always about the stage with Mack.

"That's your song," Mack shifted and Marilyn tensed in case he put his arm around her.

"I don't have a sister," Marilyn's heart ached. She knew what was coming.

"You're the sister, Marilyn. I saw you in that dress and-"

"and what? You magically knew I was a girl inside? You never said anything. I tried to tell you and you ran away. As far as I remember you wrote the song for somebody you had a crush on."

"The lyrics changed." Mack hunched his shoulders. "Haven't you noticed?"

She hadn't until this moment.

"You bastard," Marilyn made her anger push her to her feet. "You ran off all those years ago wrote a fucking song about it." She shoved her scars under his nose. "This is what not having you around did to me." Marilyn was screaming now, but she didn't care. All the pain of her abandonment poured out of her and it was beyond her power to stop.

"I going to go audition for that talent show. I'm going to win and go on tour, and every night I'm going to think of you here, worrying about making your nut."

"You can't quit," Mack said "I need you."

"No, Mack, Cher and Crysta need you. You aren't fucking that up on my account. I'm not going to be anyone's Ophelia."

She headed out the door.

"Knock 'em dead, kid," Bo said. His head lay on his arms. He was shaking, but whether from laughter or tears she couldn't tell.

PART TWO

-7-

Marilyn knocked on Anna's door the next morning.

"I'm in, but I need you to help with those forms. I'm not putting my whole life into one basket. "

"Awesome." Anna ran her fingers through her hair. "Let me get some caffeine into my system and we'll get started."

The forms weren't as bad as Marilyn expected them to be. Anna filled in most of the parts asking for why Marilyn wanted the scholarship, surgery whatever. Only one time did Marilyn stop her.

"No, I want to be a social worker to help people, not just transgendered people. It's not like you are out to help only short, perky blondes."

"True, true," Anna adjusted what she wrote. They walked to the bursar's office to drop off the scholarship forms.

"I'll mail the other one on Monday. Now I happen to know you have a paper for Professor Dingman. Apparently, I have the same paper to work on. Shoo, go write."

Marilyn walked back to her room. She tried to focus on writing the paper, but her conversation with Mack bulldozed its way into head. What was it he said at the end? *I need you.* It wasn't about him. It wasn't about Marilyn either. That's when the paper fell into place. It was to be about the underlying principle of social work which encompassed all the topics they'd covered so far. Marilyn suspected a lot of people were going to write about ethics. She would too, in her own way.

It's not about me. She wrote. As much as I enjoy being the center of attention, that isn't the place of a social worker. It is about the client's needs, decisions, rights. Those must form the

basis of our goals and objectives and it is why we must be constantly mindful....
***

"Good, Marilyn." Professor Dingman glanced at the first line of her paper. "you certainly appear to be on the right track."

She smiled as she took her seat. The student beside her leaned over.

"Awesome show at the Flying Frog." They were the first words he'd said to her since the beginning of term. Other students came up and talked to her as well. Marilyn wondered how long her new 'fame' would last since she wasn't going to be at the Frog this week. Anna and Birungi waved at her. Funny none of them moved to sit with the others. For some reason, it made her smile. Their friendship was exactly what Marilyn needed. They trusted her to survive without their constant support.

The lecture went by quickly and Marilyn went out to have coffee with

Anna and Birungi., but didn't count on the crowd that swarmed them at the Cafe. She put up with it for a while before leading the escape to her room.

"I am going to enter the show," Marilyn said, "but I need your help practicing."

"Can you not practice at the karaoke?" Birungi asked.

"I had to quit. Things weren't working out the way I'd hoped."

"Mack hit on you, didn't he?" Anna frowned.

"Something like that." Marilyn waved her hand to dismiss him. "But I need your help to focus on this show."

"All right then, what do you need?"

"I need somewhere to practice and an audience, both for my song and my backstory. Bo told me I have to get it right."

"Can't you get Bo to help you?"

"Bo's the other owner of the Frog," Marilyn said. "I'm sure of it. I quit, so I quit him too."

"Too bad." Anna stared up at the ceiling. "So what did he say about your story?"

"He seemed to think a transgendered person whose father had a heart attack and needed to spend all the family's money, including her university money, and whose parents had to sell their home and move in with her estranged brother who is an active duty Marine might be enough if I dedicated the song to my brother in the hopes of a reconciliation seven years after I last saw him."

"When you put it that way it seems overwhelming."

"It leaves out the attempted suicide and the fact he tried to kill me when I first came out as a girl."

"I can see that would be a downer."

"My boyfriend has access to a practice studio." Birungi raised her hand.

"You never mentioned a boyfriend."

"I haven't met him yet," Birungi said, "I have been so busy. His father's auntie knows a friend of my mother's. My mother and his father talked on the phone and decided Erick is allowed to talk to me. Is that not a boyfriend?"

"Close enough for me," Anna grinned and gave a thumbs up.

"Same here," Marilyn said.

"I will call him." Birungi took out a cell phone and scrolled through the numbers before tapping at one. When a voice answered, Birungi launched into a long dialog in a language Marilyn didn't recognize. Several times Birungi spoke very sharply. When she finished and hung up, she grinned at Marilyn.

"If we go there now, Erick will give me a key to the room. We can use it if we make no mess and tell no one. I am not to tell my Mother he is seeing a girl since he came here two years ago. He is not wanting to explain to his father. Erick is a musician. His father is rich and pays his fees. An angry father pays no fees."

"Birungi, you are evil," Anna said. "I like your style. Let's go." They went out a side entrance and followed Birungi along the paths to another building where a tall black man met them. He spoke rapidly with Birungi then gave her the key. Birungi led them into the building and up stairs until she walked along a hallway until they reached a room Birungi unlocked with the key.

The room was empty except for a sound system and some scattered chairs.

"Let's get started then, shall we?" Anna sat in the chair and crossed her legs. "Tell me sweetheart, why are you here?"

She worked Marilyn mercilessly.

"I've watched every season of every show. I'm addicted to these things, but I have a good idea of what will fly. A little awkwardness is endearing, but too much will make people cringe. If they do a pre-show interview, for God's sake sound humble, the people who think they are the next big thing are always buzzed. If you are going to cry, do it after you're done singing. No one wants to wait through your tears to hear if you're any good. After you're good, you'll be forgiven. Remember you are still on camera until we're well out of the building. I've seen shots following the performers right out to the street. You can't let up."

"You make it sound like I have to be totally fake the whole time," Marilyn rubbed her temples. The acting would be more work than the singing.

"Not fake, no one will buy fake. If you lie or hide stuff the webbies will tear you limb from limb."

"So I have to talk about the suicide and everything?"

"If they do a pre-show, then you may talk about the dark period in your life. On stage no, they'll know you only have so long to tell your story as long as you don't appear to hide it."

"So she should wear a shirt not quite long enough to cover the scars," Birungi put her hand on her forearm.

"Risky, but good advice. One of the softies may ask you about them. Think of what you're going to say if they do. Remember everyone else will be doing all the same things, so you need to brilliant, and carry off the back story."

When they finished with the back story, they started on the song choice.

"You need one that is well known, suits your voice and is not overdone. You do not want to be the third person in the night to sing *Feeling Good*."

"I love that song."

"Yeah, so does everyone else. We'll work up two songs just in case they decide they want you to sing something different. It doesn't happen often, but you want to be ready. It also gives you a backup if the person ahead of you steals your song."

"In Uganda, when we sing, we want the whole people to feel it," Birungi said. "Connect with the people find what they want, and give it to them."

"Hell yes." Anna nodded vigorously. "If everyone thinks you're singing just to them, they'll tear the house down for you. You can't see past the lights, but look past them like you can. Let people see your eyes and your soul."

"Bo complained this is the easy route," Marilyn sat exhausted in a chair.

"It is," Anna said, "otherwise you have to do this for years until someone pays attention."

"The audition is following the mid-term so you won't be able to go early to register."

"The mid-term is a morning one." Anna had her calendar out. "You will be able to write it and get to the audition in time."

"Erick wants to watch," Birungi put her phone away. "He will bring us in his car."

"Good to know," Anna said. "I'll look up the rules and see what you need to bring with you."

They met after class all week while Marilyn dreamed she was naked on the stage as the audience gawked and laughed at her.

***

The day of the exam, and the audition, dawned. Marilyn dressed in black pants and a white blouse Anna had approved as suitably feminine, *I don't want to look like I'm not fully dedicated to my gender of choice*, but also showed off her statuesque figure. To Anna' relief, the heels were nixed. She didn't know if she could pull them off along with everything else.

Birungi came to class with a new scarf for Marilyn and tied it carefully.

"Looking sharp for an exam, Marilyn." Professor Dingman smiled.

"I have an audition after the exam."

"Right, remember you have two hours for the exam, but no rule says you must stay the entire two hours. Good luck."

She went in and sat down. Professor Dingman told them to begin, and she flipped the page over and started answering questions. Marilyn went through them quickly, then started answering the short information based questions. They were easy. The essay questions didn't take much more time as she brought up memories of lectures and class discussion. There was one long ethics based scenario she struggled with briefly before writing her answer. She was done.

Marilyn looked up to see Anna and Birungi both gone. She rushed to the front to hand in her paper, then out to find her friends. They waited beside Erick and a girl Marilyn hadn't seen before. She jogged over and they packed into the car. Erick took off following his GPS. Marilyn's heart sank when she saw the line stretching far down the street from the theatre where they were holding the auditions.

Erick let them off and drove away to find a parking space.

"I'm so nervous," a girl just ahead of Marilyn fanned herself and sat down suddenly. Marilyn pulled her water bottle from her purse and made the girl drink it. Someone with a badge identifying themselves as a staff person for *So Sing Already Inc.* came by and Marilyn asked for more water.

"I traveled all night to get here," the girl said, "I'm just tired. I'll be fine."

"Did you eat anything?" Marilyn asked.

"I'm too nervous to eat."

"You have to eat something," Marilyn fished in her purse again. She found a granola bar and handed it to the girl. A voice in her head told her this was her competition, but Marilyn ignored it. She didn't want to win thst way.

"Is there anything you don't have in that purse?" the girl asked.

"Trade secret," Marilyn grinned. "I like big purses, the little ones make me feel gawky."

"Deanna," the girl said. "I know we're competition, but I'd rather be your friend and worry about that later."

"Marilyn." She looked around at the people chatting and laughing. A group up ahead had a pizza delivered and passed slices up and down the line. Marilyn and Deanna both ate some. The other girl's color looked a lot better.

The line moved at a crawl. Anna went off to find some food, then Tavi called Erick on her cell and went to find him. Only Birungi stood beside her when they moved into the shadow of the huge theatre. Marilyn expected to see cameras all over.

"This is the audition for the audition," Deanna said, "a friend of mine made a show last year. She had to wait ages to find out if she made the televised show, then she wasn't allowed to tell anyone. If you wear a costume you need to wear exactly the same thing. The judges even asked the same kind of questions."

"Makes sense," Marilyn sighed and squashed the dream of running out of the building with a pass to the show. "But I was kind of hoping to know today."

"You and me both."

"Contestants only past this point," a guard repeated endlessly. Birungi hugged Marilyn and followed the stream of people who headed for the doors of the theatre seating.

"Ok," the woman at the table said, "here are the releases. You can take them and read them, but no one sings until they're signed. The short version is the judges can say whatever they want about you, your appearance, your singing, as long as it isn't illegal or against company policy. That means no overt racism or sexism, but if you're dressed sexy, expect to get oggled."

Marilyn and Deanna just signed the document.

"I didn't come all this way to go away without singing," Deanna said. Marilyn nodded. They followed the line to the next table were the staff pinned or taped numbers to the front of the contestants.

"If you're taking off any portion of your costume, please make sure you don't remove your number until after you start singing." The woman pinned the number to Marilyn's blouse. "Lovely scarf, darling" she said before she went back to her scripted sentence and pinned the number on the person behind her

They were called into side rooms in groups where they got to sing accapella for a few seconds while bored looking people at a table made notes. They handed papers to ushers who sent some people out one door and others through a second one. Marilyn was sent through the second door to join another line which snaked up the stairs to a big room full of contestants.

"All right," another person walked in to talk to them. "here's how it works. You walk out onto the stage and you get five seconds to get ready. Then your music starts, double check your backing file is the one you want before you go out on the stage. Do overs make the judges grumpy. After you've sung, the judges may or may not comment on your performance. We have a limited number of direct passes. That means a guaranteed spot on the live auditions. It doesn't mean a guaranteed pass through the live auditions. If you get a pass we ask you don't post it on social media. If it shows up before the live auditions, your pass will be revoked. This show is about singing, people, so sing. Some footage is being shot today and may be used on the live show if the producers feel it's appropriate. From this point on, you may be called out of numerical sequence so we don't get a long run of similar acts. If you made it this far, you will not go home without singing on the big stage. Try to relax and if you need to puke, use the garbage cans placed around the studio. We will let you wave off one call to sing, but not two. Questions?"

She waved them into the studio. The odor of nerves hit Marilyn, but nothing else. Either no one puked, or they cleaned up quickly. She looked down at her chest.

"Deanna, What's my number?"

"You're 19783, what am I?"

"19782," Marilyn grinned suddenly. "We made it, we're really here."

"Yep, we are." Deanna gave Marilyn a quick hug. "I wouldn't have made it without you. Even if I don't make it a step further, it was worth it to meet you."

Marilyn wandered aimlessly in the studio humming softly to warm up her voice. She sang a few soft scales and they blended with the sounds others warming up around her. The unconscious music made her shiver.

"782, then 783. You're up" the woman called through the studio. She waved them over. You have your thumb drive?" she asked, "only one file on the drive?"

Marilyn and Deanna nodded.

"Good, pass the drive to the computer guy. Wait to see that it is the correct file before you walk out on stage."

They nodded again and moved up to the stage. Deanna handed her drive to the tech. She looked at the screen to check and gave a thumbs up. The contestant before them buzzed out after a few seconds of nasal, not quite in tune singing. Marilyn handed her thumb drive to the tech.

Then Deanna started singing.

"Me, and my shadow..."

She had a glorious clear voice which carried the song to the rafters. It was the same song Marilyn had planned to sing.

"I need to change my song," she whispered to the tech.

"Sorry," the tech said, "we only can change the backing tune for an error, like if we got someone else's thumb drive. We can't let you change your mind. Isn't the first time its happened."

"Can you just not play any music at all?"

"Don't see why not," the man shrugged, "It's your funeral."

"I won the last competition where the tech guy said that to me."

"Well good luck then."

"So," one of the judges spoke. Marilyn could only see vague shapes, "tell me about yourself."

"I traveled all night to get here," Deanna said, "and I almost passed out in line."

"I hope one of our staff took care of you,"

"One of the contestants did. She gave me her water and food and everything."

"Sounds like an angel," the judge responded.

"I think so."

"We'll hope she sings like one."

The next judge commented about how beautifully Deanna sang and pulled from her that she was a farm girl and home schooled, but she wanted to sing for a living.

Deanna bounced off the stage and hugged Marilyn. They danced in circles for a few seconds, before the woman with the clipboard cleared her throat. She grinned at them.

"Now that's television," a man's voice muttered from behind Marilyn.

"Five seconds from when you hit the mark," the clipboard woman pointed out onto the stage.

Marilyn tapped her hand against her leg as she walked.

She entered the circle.

One, she breathed in,

Two,

Three, she breathed out

Four

Five, she breathed in and began to sing.

-8-

"Sitting on the dock of the bay..." she sang. She let a little rasp into her voice to match the song. It was low for her tenor voice, but she hoped the sound carried out to the audience. It was too late to grab the mic. No one had said if they were allowed to. Neither the girl before or Deanna had. She kept her hand tapping to the music in her head as she let the song carry her away. She tried to look out at the audience. She couldn't see anything, but heard some cheers. They grew as she let her voice swell into the chorus and then the bridge. The audience carried her higher, then drop to silence at the end with the whistle, as close to the mic as she could get.

The last note echoed as her hand stopped tapping.

There was a moment of silence. Then the theatre erupted. Marilyn enjoyed the applause at the Flying Frog and even the jokes at the University talent show, but this transported her. She put her head back and laughed while tears ran down her face. If she never moved on, she'd remember this moment with a smile the rest of her life.

"Two in a row," one of the judges said, "What are the odds?"

"Where did that voice come from?" another judge asked. Even from here on stage they were little more than blurs.

"I want to dedicate my song to my brother, who's a Marine on active duty," Marilyn spoke up. Anna's voice in her head coached her. *Careful, don't let the judges think you have an agenda.* "I haven't seen him since he left our home seven years ago because he couldn't understand his baby brother really was a girl inside." Emotion hit her hard and she couldn't hold back the sob that shook her. The audience's reaction caressed her.

"You're hoping he'll talk to you now?"

"I hope so," Marilyn pushed the words past the tears."

"Where are your parents, sweetheart?" the woman judged asked.

"They're living with Brent on base," Marilyn said, "My Dad had a heart attack, and we didn't have insurance so we lost everything."

"What do you do for a living?" That was the one on the end. The one who exclaimed about finding two singers in a row.

"I was a waitress at the Flying Frog." *Hope that helps, Mack,* "but I had to quit to audition."

"Why wouldn't they let you audition?" *Oops, that didn't sound good.*

"They encouraged me, and helped me find my voice, but I didn't have time to work, rehearse and go to school."

"You're doing all that?" it was the woman again.

"I can't quit. I almost quit once, and I promised my parents I'd never do it again."

"It must have been hard, coming out, losing your brother, becoming a different person."

"You have no idea," Marilyn said, "but what kept me going was I wasn't becoming a different person. I was becoming me."

The audience erupted again.

"I'm sure you don't need us to tell you that you have a lovely voice, and such a daring choice of song."

Marilyn walked off the stage into Deanna's arms.

"They wanted me to leave, but I wasn't going until you sang. I've never heard anything like it." She continued to chatter at Marilyn as they walked arm in arm down the corridor.

"You can't write stuff like this," Marilyn heard behind her, but she didn't care. She came, she sang, they loved her.

Her friends mobbed her as she left the theatre. Somehow they fit Deanna in the car and went off to a restaurant to celebrate.

Marilyn convinced Deanna to spend the night in her room, before she had to take the bus home the next morning. She didn't think about the problem of getting changed for bed with a stranger in the room. She hadn't let anyone see her naked since she started the hormones and felt even more awkward about her body. She solved the problem by falling on her bed fully clothed and dropping into an immediate sleep.

She woke up before Deanna and went to the showers to clean up and change. She had no exams today, so the only thing she needed to worry about was getting Deanna to the bus. She sat down to check her email. There was something from *So Sing Already Inc.*

Congratulations, you've been selected as one of the limited number of guaranteed passes to the live auditions. This in no way implies that you will get through the audition to the next level. You are reminded that any posting of this information on social media will result in the revoking of the pass. Make sure you preserve what clothes you wore at the audition for the live audition. Look at the dates and clear your schedule. It is easier to reschedule now than at the last minute. Once the audience voting starts only extreme emergencies will be cause for contestants to leave the campus. Some contestants may be selected for pre-show interviews, being selected for a pre-show interview does not guarantee a passage to the next level. The contract you signed includes permission for us to contact people you mentioned in your biography and to validate the details of your biography. Good luck!

Marilyn's squeal woke Deanna.

"You're up already?"

"I thought you grew up on a farm." Marilyn said.

"Just because I have to get up early, doesn't mean I like it. Why do you think I want to become a singer?"

"Right, bathrooms down the hall." Deanna wandered out. When she came back a few minutes later, her hair was wet and she looked more awake.

"Wow, this is luxury when you grow up in a family of twelve." She shook her head. "I guess I'd better get the phone call over with. Papa is not going to be happy. Where can I make a call?"

"Use my phone," Marilyn handed her the phone. She helped Deanna dial the number, then stepped out to give her a little privacy. She went back into the room when she heard sobs through the door.

"They won't let me come back." Deanna sat slumped on the floor. "They told me I made my choice and could live with it."

"I'll find you somewhere here. You can find a job and survive until the next stage of the show."

"There's no guarantee," Deanna said

Marilyn pointed at the computer.

"If they gave me a pass, they had to have given you one."

Deanna put her hand over her mouth. For a second, Marilyn thought she was going to faint.

"We're in?"

"We can't tell anyone." Marilyn put her finger to her lips. "No one,"

Deanna bobbed her head, then began dancing around the room. Marilyn laughed and joined in. Marilyn dragged Deanna downstairs for breakfast with Anna and Blrungi.

After breakfast they had a strategy meeting.

"First thing is to find a place for Deanna to crash. The University won't be happy if we try to stash her in our rooms." Anna drank the last of her coffee. "There are people who rent to students, but they're likely full up."

"What about the Y or something?" Marilyn said, "How old are you? Maybe there's a youth shelter."

"I'm eighteen," Deanna said, "I don't want a place with lots of rules. I can't be turning down late shifts because I have curfew."

"Makes sense," Anna tapped her finger on the table. "What about the Flying Frog, for a job? They'll be looking for a server again."

"They owe me," Marilyn said, "we'll go down at lunch. Mack won't be there."

"I'd love to meet your friends." Deanna smiled broadly.

They took Deanna on a short walking tour of the city. Then Marilyn walked Deanna to the Flying Frog. It wasn't a place she ever expected to enter again.

"Marilyn?" Cher ran over to her. "Bo wouldn't let me call you, but he's real sick. He can't walk from the shakes."

"I'll go see him in a second." Marilyn pushed her fear aside. "Cher, this is Deanna. She's looking for a job and if you know of a cheap place to stay."

"You have any serving experience?" Cher asked.

"I grew up with twelve siblings," Deanna shrugged.

Cher rolled her eyes and made pushing motions with her hands. Marilyn walked to the door and knocked on it. Something that might have been *come in* came through the door so she pushed the door open.

Whatever Marilyn expected it wasn't what she saw. Bo lay on a bed in a room as antiseptic and bare as a hospital room.

"Heh," Bo said, "When you live on the road you don't collect much stuff, or people."

"Cher told me you were sick."

"Yeah, well, I've been sick for a while," Bo put out his hand and Marilyn pulled him to a sitting position. "You're a strong lass, got your new plumbing yet?"

"No," Marilyn sat beside him. Just weeks ago he was a force of nature, now he could barely sit on his own. "I did OK at the audition, actually I did better than that. The whole place was on their feet."

"Better than sex, heh?" Bo said. "It's more addictive than any drug, and it will kill you just as dead. Enjoy it, kid, you earned it. It won't get much better than this."

"I couldn't have done it without you." Marilyn hugged him.

She left Deanna with Cher and walked down the long hill to the docks. The pungent fish and seaweed suited her mood. She hated seeing Bo like he was. All the fire had gone out of him. She imagined herself living in an empty room in the back of a bar and shuddered.

"I won't end up there," she said to the seagulls. They just screamed at her and flew away.

She took the bus up the hill. She saw people sitting against buildings as others stepped over them. A lot of them were young, some were old. With the wrong kind of luck, that could be Bo or Deanna.

Or in a few months, Marilyn. She shuddered again and ran her song through her head. She'd eat sleep and breathe the music until she owned it.

When she got back to university, she went to her room and slept like the dead.

***

"One thing you will learn quickly as social workers is people don't care about your intentions. They want action, and they want results." Professor Dingman paced the room and lectured while Marilyn tried not to let her attention wander to the pile of graded exams sitting face down on his desk. "This is why your bosses will want you to fill out endless statistics. They show in part the results of your work. Not all results are easily measured by statistics. So, what things may be objectives that are not quantifiable? Marilyn?"

"Contentment?" Marilyn guessed. He so rarely called on students that she was never ready for it.

"So how would you find out if your clients were more or less content?"

"I'd ask them."

"Very good, self-reporting of clients is a good way to start. Anything else?"

"Maybe see if the number of times they complained changed, or what they complained about?"

"Interesting," Professor Dingman waved his hand at them. "It is worth considering, how you measure the unmeasurable. If you get into research, there are whole papers on the subject. Fortunately for me, and for most of you. I have an easily quantifiable way of measuring your learning. Don't panic if the mark is not what you expected, this is only worth twenty percent of your final grade. The final exam and essay together are worth sixty. There is time yet to improve. Because I like to recognize excellence I will hand out the first five papers in order of their grade. Papers after that are in no particular order."

"Birungi," he waved a paper in the air.

"Anna."

"Cameron,"

Marilyn's test wasn't in the top five, but she was pleased with the 'B' she received, her highest mark so far in the course.

"You got the highest grade?" Anna didn't quite glare at Birungi as they drank their coffee.

"Mother made me report on my learning each week when she called me on the computer. Translating into

Lusoga and explaining to Mother is good study."

"I will have to try that."

"You know Lusoga?" Birungi lifted her eyebrow.

"Not yet," Anna said.

Birungi broke into a long speech in her language.

"What did you say?" Marilyn asked.

"That it is Anna's turn to fetch the coffee," Birungi said with a bright smile.

-9-

"Perception is reality." Professor Dingman paced the room and scratched notes on the board, apparently oblivious to the camera crew filming the lecture. Marilyn wondered if he'd chosen the subject for deliberate irony. "This is a common saying in the counseling field suggesting the client's perception of their situation is their reality. It is foolish then to attempt to treat the client outside of that reality. One of the main tasks of clinical social work is to empower the client to broaden their perception. On occasion, just a broadened perception is enough to set the client on a new path to a healthier life. Yet we'd be remiss to say perception is reality only applies to the clinical social work field. How might you need to address the concept in a community setting?"

"If you are bringing diverse communities together," Cameron said, "the perceptions and prejudgments the communities have of each other will get in the way."

Marilyn took a deep breath.

"The not-in-my-backyard reaction to everything from halfway homes to new development is a problem of perception. But the issue of perception is reality is not only a group's perception of other groups but their perception of themselves. If you try to put a women's shelter in a community that doesn't see itself as having any violence against women issues you will get a much stronger backlash than in a community which sees the shelter as lowering property values."

She sat back in her seat and focused on looking attentive to the other students. The only concession to having the cameras present was a brief announcement the week before that any student who didn't want to appear on camera would be excused from the class.

Marilyn had never seen so many people in the class before. The crew had sat down with the professor and Marilyn to discuss the filming. They wanted the Professor to feed her the question.

"Reality doesn't need a script," he'd said and refused to budge.

They wanted her to speak specifically on transgender rights.

"I'm transgender." Marilyn crossed her arms. "But as a social worker I will work with people of all populations, I can't be about just one group no matter how connected I am with them." She refused to move on that. The crew muttered but the contract didn't require Marilyn to read from a script, just to cooperate.

Filming in other parts of the university created different problems. Birungi refused to appear on camera. She didn't think her mother would approve. Anna gave a brilliant and touching interview on how she'd moved from seeing Marilyn as a subject of investigation to a friend. Several students Marilyn had never met tried to claim to be her boyfriend/girlfriend. One student announced they were intersexed and was both.

"We're used to this," the crew chief told Marilyn. As soon as someone gets a little fame, everyone wants to hop on board for the ride. I've worked for other shows and I'm good at weeding out the kooks. If I'm not sure, I'll check with you."

"Look at this," Anna leaned back from the computer. They were hiding out in Anna's room to escape the people who wanted to bask in Marilyn's fame. "You're on YouTube."

Marilyn and Birungi leaned over Anna's shoulder and watched a shaky video of Marilyn singing karaoke at the Flying Frog.

"That's the night after the University show," Marilyn said. "They were crazy. I actually got scared."

"You don't appear scared," Birungi moved closer to the screen.

"Looks are deceiving." Marilyn fought back tears. That was the night she'd screamed at Mack. He didn't deserve it, but she hadn't found the courage to talk to him.

There were videos of all her songs from that night, including the set where she played drums.

"Holy shit," Anna turned up the volume. "Listen to the words from THAT fourth song."

"Yeah," Marilyn closed her eyes and sighed. "*Do you have a sister?* is what Mack called it. He wrote it years back for an older girl who he had a crush on. Then it was about a younger sister who might give him the time of day. He apparently changed the words."

"Well they are now seriously creepy," Anna said. "It's like he fell in love with a female version of you."

"He pretty much did, according to him. Things might have been so different if he hadn't moved away, but maybe not."

"Let's see what other stuff is out there." Anna typed in Marilyn's name into Google and Marilyn gasped as how much came up.

"I'm not officially famous yet. Where is all this coming from?"

"A lot of it is from a piece written by a girl named Tuni," Anna clicked on a link. "She's a real firecracker. Look at this video."

Marilyn watched the video of Tuni confronting Mr. Hall in the school parking lot. A student had posted it right after the event. They watched the interview with Tuni and read the article.

"Who is this girl?" Anna asked. "She looks like she's twelve."

"Yeah, she got that a lot," Marilyn grinned as memories returned. "Tuni was the very first person who just took me as I was without trying to put me in a box. She's also the smartest person I've ever met. No offense, guys, but she scored perfect on all her exams. That was after someone tried to rape her, after she ended up in hospital with smoke inhalation from a fire in chemistry, after the entire school, including most of the teachers ostracized her for becoming my friend. Then she went to the board and wrote all the exams for the next term and walked away from school. She's on internship with some internet magazine here in Seattle."

"Let's type in her name and see what comes up." Anna's fingers flew over the keys.

"Oh wow," Marilyn looked at the list of articles. Homelessness in Seattle; the cumulative hits people took with addictions, mental illness, poverty. Tuni had seen the same people on the sidewalk as Marilyn had, but she didn't turn away. She bounced around from there, writing on economics, on human rights. The last few months she'd been in India with a magazine there writing on women's rights. Marilyn noticed a paper on how Indian society perceived transgendered people differently. The most recent article was on poverty among foreign students in Seattle. "She's home?" Marilyn scrambled for her phone. "I have to call her. You guys will love her."

"You go have dinner with her and reconnect first," Anna put her hand on Marilyn's shoulder. "Then we'll all go out. We don't want to make you uncomfortable. It's been almost a year since you saw her last. You'll need to adjust."

Birungi nodded and smiled.

"I look forward to meeting your friend, she sounds most interesting."

Marilyn beamed at her friends.

"You guys are amazing, you know that, don't you?" She dialed Tuni's number and counted the rings.

"Hello," Tuni's voice still had the rasp making her sound like a soprano Lurch.

"Hi Tuni, it's Marilyn. I'm taking courses at the University in Seattle. You up for supper?"

"Of course," Tuni said. "I was planning to call you myself, I bumped into a friend of yours."

"Where do you want to meet?"

"There's a nice little Indian buffet not far from the University." Tuni gave directions and they agreed on a time.

Marilyn walked to the restaurant with butterflies in her stomach. Waiting for the audition hadn't been as nerve wracking. How much had Tuni changed? What if she didn't care about Marilyn anymore? The breadth of Tuni's world took Marilyn's breath away. While Marilyn was struggling through the final term of high school, Tuni was out trying to change the world. A large part of why Marilyn came to Seattle was the hope of reconnecting with Tuni, but she hadn't sent an email or tried to phone until she saw her friend on the internet.

Marilyn stopped on the sidewalk. Why was she afraid of her friend?

"Hi Marilyn," Tuni said, and Marilyn had to look around to see the woman with the wide grin on her face. The next second they were hugging tight.

"Let me look at you. I almost didn't recognize you."

"Yeah, it's nice not to look like I'm twelve." Tuni grinned. "A doctor in India helped with some hormones and diet. He couldn't make me taller though. I see I'm not the only one to have changed."

"I started the hormones right after you left. I should have started earlier, but I was angry and wanted to punish the school board."

"The things we do to ourselves." Tuni shook her head. "Let's go eat." She put her arm through Marilyn's and they walked to where the scent of curry wafted onto the street.

Dinner was amazing, though Marilyn might have eaten cardboard and not cared. Tuni wanted to hear all about John Wayne.

"He was sweet," Marilyn said, "but we were going in opposite directions. He had a crush on my guy body, and I was growing breasts. We had fun, but I think we both knew it was never going to go anywhere. He's playing football down east and having a great time."

"Yeah, he emailed me when he was accepted into the University on a full ride no less. So, here you are in Seattle." Tuni tilted her head and looked at Marilyn.

"I think I wanted to prove I could manage without your help." Marilyn poked at her food. "That last term at Punky's Hound's no one would say boo to me, but they weren't lining up to be friends either. I wasn't anathema, but I wasn't accepted either. I needed to find out whether I could do this myself."

"So tell me about life in Seattle," Tuni put her hand on Marilyn's.

"You already figured that out," Marilyn raised her eyebrows, not really surprised.

"Not really," Tuni said. "Not in those terms, I knew you'd call when the time was right. I didn't want to intrude on your life, but I must admit I was planning to bump into you any day now. I heard from Erick you auditioned for a talent show and a film crew came to campus?" She waggled her eyebrow a little and Marilyn laughed.

"It's been a little crazy. I decided I had to enter to pay for school..." She told

Tuni about the phone call and her panic over money, the decision to enter the show. Tuni laughed at the scientific manner in which Anna had groomed Marilyn's story.

"So, you are going to sing again to for the show?"

"This time for the celebrity judges," Marilyn said. "For a live show, they use a lot of scripting and maybe clips from the first auditions. I don't know how I'll react the second time. We wrote a script for me to follow, but my reactions weren't fake."

"I suspect you just need to be genuine and you will do great," Tuni squeezed Marilyn's hand. "It sounds like Anna has everything in hand, so I am going to relegate myself to being your greatest fan."

"It is so good to see you," Marilyn squeezed back. "I don't know why I didn't do this sooner."

"Yeah, you do," Tuni said, "but I'm really glad you made the call."

"So, what have you been doing?"

"A little of this, a little of that. I'm finding it hard to focus on one thing. I'm like a super-genius with a five-minute attention span. Look, a squirrel. The editors at *New Economy* have been understanding, but I think they are getting frustrated. The trip to India was supposed to help me pick one thing and stick with it, but even there I was all over the place. I have stories around gurus and changes in caste and the challenges of bridging into modernity from a society that has seen very little change in some regions in centuries. I want to go to university, but I can't bear to pick just one thing to learn. I want to learn all of it."

"So why not?" Marilyn asked. "Why do you have to pick? It would be a waste of your talents if you did just one thing. You aren't everybody else, Tuni. I'm sure there are other people as smart as you out there, but I've never met one. Your problem is you are trying to be average because the world is made for average people. Stop worrying about being average. If *New Economy* wants focused articles, write those ones, and write the other ones for yourself or another magazine."

"You'd think if I was so smart, I'd have figured if out for myself." Tuni laughed, but Marilyn was sure there were tears in her eyes.

-10-

"The challenge of living in a world in which perception is reality; is we make our own reality, then have a very hard time seeing outside of that reality." Professor Dingman didn't have any cameras this week, and the class shrank to its normal size "Even well-educated and intelligent people find it difficult to get past their biases. It affects the way we do research, how we counsel people and the assumptions we make about the communities we are trying to develop."

"So, what do we do?" Anna asked, "How do we see past something we don't know is there?"

"Ask a friend," Marilyn said, "or a colleague. Talk to as many different people as possible and listen for the things that don't match your worldview. That's probably your bias. It's like dirt on a window. We don't see the window, but we see the dirt."

"What did you put in your coffee?" Anna asked, "That's brilliant."

"I had supper with a super-genius." Marilyn grinned and shrugged. "Maybe a little rubbed off."

"As it happens, you are correct, Marilyn." The professor broke into the exchange. "It is the reason journals are peer reviewed, though it isn't perfect, it is also why we have supervision. Our biggest task as social workers is not fixing the client, or the world. It is seeing how our own assumptions and expectations get in the way of what we need to do. It is very easy once we start working to stop being mindful of our biases..."

Marilyn listened to Professor Dingman's lecture with one ear while she wondered what biases she carried were getting in the way. It didn't help that the reading suggested one's bias was essential to functioning in the world. It was too much work to constantly reassess all the information coming in, so filters removed most of it.

"All right then," Professor Dingman wrapped up the class. "I will remind you your final paper is due next week. If you have any problems or questions, come and see me. The exam is the week following. Next week will be an opportunity to ask whatever questions you have from the term and I will attempt to answer them all in two hours."

Anna and Birungi led the way to the Cafe where they had coffee and plotted.

"We need to get you into that practice space and keep you sharp." Anna tapped her finger on the table. "You don't want to come apart at the audition for lack of practice."

"You're right. Birungi, do you think Erick would let us in again?"

"He's been asking if we need the space." Birungi flashed a grin. "He is most eager to be helpful."

"Great," Anna said, "the sooner the better."

"I do need to study for the exam and write a paper." Marilyn pointed out.

"We'll take it easy on you until after the paper." Anna drank her coffee. "But the timing's tight."

"I have most of the paper done," Marilyn said, "I just need to polish it."

"She'll be passing us for top of the class." Anna peered into her cup and pushed it away with a sigh.

"Mother has been most interested in the direction my paper Ohas taken," Birungi gave Anna an evil grin.

"I suppose I'd better start," Anna said.

Birungi pulled out her phone and called Erick.

"When do we get to meet your super-genius friend?" Anna asked as Birungi spoke on her phone.

"Tomorrow night," Marilyn said, "at the Indian buffet if you are up for Indian."

"Sounds good."

"Erick says we can use the studio now if we wish."

"Let's go."

The practice session left Marilyn exhausted and feeling very cynical. She knew she was manipulating people's perceptions of her, playing with their biases. It was too easy. She told herself it was in a good cause; the money would pay for her next term and she was no closer to getting any other way. Instead, she felt further away from her goal. While she'd had a job, she put away some money. That little nest egg was gone. Now she needed to win this contest, or she'd be out of school next term.

Supper with Tuni distracted her from her funk. Anna and Birungi clicked with her immediately. Birungi had Tuni laughing with stories of her mother and the difficulties of translating concepts into her first language. Tuni talked about her experiences learning Hindi and some of the mistakes she'd made. Anna mostly listened, but at one point she winked at Marilyn. She looked at her friends and wondered how she got so lucky.

Her phone buzzed and she almost didn't answer it. Habit prevailed and she glanced at the text.

Bo wants to see you.

Bad?

Dying.

"I've got to go," Marilyn said her voice catching. "I'm sorry, but Bo needs me."

"Go," Tuni and Anna responded at the same time.

"I will walk with you," Birungi stood up.

Marilyn had to force herself to walk slowly so Birungi didn't have to run to keep up.

"Death is hard," Birungi said.

"How do you know he's dying?"

"What else would make you drop everything and run to his side?" Birungi sighed and looked up at Marilyn. "I've seen how you talk of him. It will be very hard for you."

"Yeah," Marilyn said, "he's rude and horrible, but I love him like he was my grandfather. He never once cared about what I was, just how hard I worked at learning what he taught me."

"I will leave you here," Birungi hugged Marilyn outside the door. "Don't be afraid to tell him the truth."

Marilyn pushed the door of the Flying Frog open and saw Cher sitting at the table crying while Mack held her. He just nodded his head towards Bo's room. Marilyn walked in. Deanna mopped Bo's forehead.

"I'll leave you to talk." She left with the basin and facecloth.

"I heard you wanted to talk to me," Marilyn said.

"I'm dying, kid," Bo rasped, "about fucking time too."

Marilyn laughed and sat beside him.

"Trust you to be cantankerous to the end."

"It's who I am. No need to change it now. I didn't want have you come and weep all over me. I wanted to warn you."

"About what? You've told me the dangers of the business enough."

"Not just that." Bo coughed and frowned. "That angelic friend of yours. She's trouble."

"Has she done anything to you?"

"What could she do? Besides, I'm no threat to her. You are. I can't tell you what it is, maybe it's just my cynical nature, but she's a player. I know, like calls to like."

"I'll be careful," Marilyn said.

"The other thing is, don't make me any promises."

"What?"

"People do it all the time, *I'll win this for Bo.* and shit like that. If you're going to win, win for yourself. I'll be dead."

"If I had my new plumbing," Marilyn's heart cracked. "I'd be by to let you test drive it."

"I'm a dirty old man, kid."

"Yes, you are, but I love you for it." Marilyn leaned down and kissed him on the cheek.

"Hell, if I'd known you were that easy, I'd have paid for it myself."

Marilyn laughed and rubbed her hand through his hair. Tears burned in her eyes. but she didn't care.

"Go, take care of yourself," Bo said, "I'm a stubborn old cuss, I may get to vote for you yet." Marilyn kissed him lightly on the lips. Then stood up and turned away. Bo wouldn't want her seeing the tears in his eyes.

"Whatever happens, kid," she heard from behind her, "I'll make sure you're OK,"

Out in the main room, Deanna hugged her, then went back into the room with Bo.

"Marilyn," Mack said, "you were right, about everything. You are always welcome here."

Cher nodded at her. Marilyn hugged both of them, then headed out into the night. She walked to the University wrapped up in her thoughts. She didn't see her friends, until she closed the door.

"You didn't think we were going to let you be alone, did you?" Anna said.

"How did you get in?" Marilyn asked.

"You left your purse at the restaurant," Tuni waved Marilyn's huge bag.

"Tell us of your friend," Birungi pulled Marilyn to sit beside her on the bed.

"It was awful," Marilyn spoke in a monotone. "He couldn't sit up. He knew he was dying and was mad he wasn't dead yet, but he wanted to live long enough to vote for me. He also told me Deanna was a player. She's been taking care of him all this time.

"It doesn't hurt to check her out," Anna shrugged.

"True, but it doesn't matter," Marilyn waved her hand. "It isn't like there is anything she could do before the audition. We're a pair, she needs me as much as I need her."

"But later," Tuni said, "you'll be competitors. You will be all the more dangerous to her since you are so close."

"You guys sound so serious." Marilyn didn't want to think about Deanna. "Bo could be imagining things."

"Has Bo been wrong before?" Birungi hugged her. "It is foolish to have a teacher and not listen."

"Leave Deanna to us," Anna said. "You keep being the open, trusting person everyone loves. That way we've got it covered both ways."

***

Erick showed them into a different practice studio.

"The other one is busy. This is better."

Anna walked around the room. Where the other room was empty but for the player and the chairs this had recording equipment and mixing boards and computers up against the wall.

"Just singing today," Anna whispered as she passed Marilyn.

They worked on Marilyn's song and Marilyn worked through a few songs she might use if she got through. She was exhausted by the end of the session. Anna gave the key back to Erick and thanked him for his help.

"Call me paranoid," Anna said, "but we practice your story work in my room from now on."

Marilyn was too tired to argue.

She woke up in the night to a red glow. It came from her computer. Marilyn got up to get a drink of water and shut the lid of the computer. The glow disappeared, and she returned to bed.

She called the Flying Frog, and Cher told her there was no change in Bo. Marilyn opened her computer and the red light came back on. Closing the computer, Marilyn went to talk to Anna.

"The red light means your web cam is active," Anna frowned and tapped her finger on her leg. "Have you used Skype or anything like that?"

"No, who would I talk to? All my friends are here."

"I have a hacker friend; let's get her to look at your computer."

The friend didn't fit Marilyn's concept of hacker. She looked more like an athlete than someone who hunched over a keyboard all day.

"Computers are old news." Babs sat down in front of Marilyn's laptop. "Most of the interesting stuff is done with cell phones now. Every year we get some bozo hacking into computers in the women's dorms and activating web cams in hopes of getting their rocks off. Stupid when you think of it. How much time do you spend naked in front of the computer?" She typed a few commands into things Marilyn had never seen. "I've disabled the webcam and microphone for you. If someone breaks through that, you have a serious issue. Call me and we'll track them down and explain some facts of life to them."

"What about your computer?" Marilyn asked after Babs left.

"Babs has already been through it and she'll look at Birungi's as well."

"Where did you meet her?" Marilyn asked.

"Old girlfriend," Anna said. "We went to school together."

"I'm glad you're still on speaking terms. So I can work on my essay in peace. Whoopee."

Anna laughed and left.

Marilyn handed in her paper and listened to Professor Dingman answer questions from the class. He blushed and smiled when they applauded him at the end.

"I don't normally watch these shows," the professor told her after class, "but I must admit I am looking forward to seeing you sing. Having said that, I hope you don't give up on social work. However much talent you have as a singer, I think you have at least as much as a social worker. Good luck."

The exam came as an anti-climax. Marilyn found it no more difficult than the mid-term. Nothing remained between her and the audition but time.

-11-

Marilyn showed up at the theatre fifteen minutes ahead of the time she was told to be there. It looked like everyone else had as well. She wandered up and down the line looking for Deanna. The other girl didn't show until just before the time given.

"The old coot is still hanging in," Deanna whispered to Marilyn. "He'll get to see you on TV."

"Thanks, Deanna. I'm sorry I didn't get over there more to see you."

"You have school and stuff. I get it."

"Listen up people." A woman with a megaphone walked out the door and got their attention. "We have a few set pieces with the celebrity judges arriving. No big deal, just look enthusiastic. After that we will get you to come in and pick up your packages at the registration table. There will be dressing rooms to change into your costume if you need to do so. You will get the same numbers you had before and will perform in more or less the same sequence. Don't worry about trying to duplicate everything from the previous audition. The judges will have their own questions and they may be different from what you answered last time. Remember this is still an audition even though you are on TV

"All the same rules apply as last time. You are responsible for your own music. You get five seconds from hitting the mark and you sing. No do overs if you miss your cue, so pay attention and stay sharp. We want a good show here, but keep it real.

"We're going to be awhile," Deanna pointed to the table with water set up. "I've learned my lesson." They grabbed a water each and tried to relax. Marilyn talked with part of her attention while her music ran in the back of her head. The waiting wasn't any easier this time.

The warm ups around them created the same discordant background as the first audition. Marilyn wondered why it was in a minor key this time. They moved slowly up the line to where they were watching the performer on stage. It wasn't the nasally singer who'd been buzzed last time, but this person didn't do much better. He sang like his mouth was full of golf balls.

Deanna checked her music and gave the thumbs up. She ran out to the mark and Marilyn counted the five seconds to the music starting. That glorious voice carried her away again. Deanna sang to the audience like a pro; she had them in the palm of her hand by the end of the song. The judges had to wait for the applause to die down before they asked her the same questions asked last time and Deanna answered with little variation. This time she talked of being disowned for wanting a career in music, and Marilyn was made to look even more angelic. The judges complimented her singing and gave her all yeses. Deanna bounced back and they hugged again. Marilyn fought the deja vu, she couldn't lose focus. There was no issue with the music this time. The tech was a woman this time who gave her a thumbs up. Marilyn took a breath and made sure her throat was clear, then she starting tapping her finger and walked out to the mark.

Breathe in, breath out, breath in.

Sing.

Marilyn had worried whether she could duplicate the experience of the first audition, but the crowd was with her from the start. She used the mic better to get the low notes out and even over the screaming she heard her big notes come back to her. She leaned close in to whistle the last phrase and the theatre fell silent as the final sound faded. Then the judges and the audience were on their feet and Marilyn thought of Bo and laughed through her tears.

She could get used to this.

"Where did you come from?" the first judge asked.

"If I can," Marilyn said, "I'd like to dedicate my song to my brother who's an active Marine."

"Sure, darling," one of the woman judges said. "It has to be hard to have a brother who's away that much."

"Actually, I haven't seen him in seven years. Not since the first time I came out as a girl."

"So, you're hoping this will reconcile you?"

"I really hope so," A catch in Marilyn's throat caught her. *What might her life have been like with Brent at her side?*

"Where did you learn to sing like that?" That was the first judge, perhaps a little annoyed she hadn't answered his question.

"Karaoke night at the Flying Frog," Marilyn answered. "The people there are like family to me." She already dedicated the song to Brent, but she sent out a personal dedication to Bo.

"What about your family?" the judge asked, "Are they here tonight?"

"I hope they're watching, but my parents had to move in with my brother after a heart attack cost them all their savings."

"So what are you doing?" That was the judge on the end.

"Studying social work." Let's keep things simple this time.

"And how are you paying for school?"

"That's why I'm here." Marilyn grinned at the judges.

They commented more on her singing and the choice to sing without music. One judge complained the tapping of her finger was distracting, but the others booed him down. In the end, she got all yeses and she was able to run into

Deanna's hug before they danced together down the corridor.

Someone at the door handed her a phone.

"Hello?" Marilyn said.

"Hey sis," a voice same through a crackle on the connection. "The brass told me I should give you a call. Something about an audition?"

"That's right, Brent. I sang a song for you."

"I was a stupid kid, Marilyn. When I get back to the States I want to come and see you."

"Anytime," Marilyn whispered.

"Good luck with the audition."

"I made it through, Brent. I'm in the next round."

"That's fantastic," Brent's excitement somehow came through the static. "Love you, sis."

Marilyn whispered goodbye and realized she was on her knees weeping while the cameras recorded. She didn't care. She had her brother back.

Her friends came and swept her away from the cameras and the crowds. Anna made an unusual number of turns before they pulled into a parking lot of an all-night Denny's.

Nobody recognized her and it took a moment to register that not every TV was tuned to *So Sing Already*. She had a chance to pull herself together before life got crazy.

"You did great," Anna said, after they gave their orders to the server. "even better than the first one. It helps to have an educated audience. This is where the interviews and stuff will help you. We'll talk through some of that when you're ready.

"What happened at the end where you collapsed?" Tuni asked.

"My brother phoned." Marilyn felt the tears again. "Someone told him to call.

He wants to meet up when he's back in the states."

"They're pulling strings already." Anna drank from her water. "The show probably got permission to talk to him. That scene was dramatic enough it's sure to run."

"I thought the show was live." Marilyn's stomach churned at the thought of the world listening into that dialogue.

"There's live and then there's live," Anna shrugged and played with her glass. "They'll have a delay to manage things like redoes and technical glitches. They'd already have the clips they wanted to show for different people. You didn't have a space between when Deanna sang and when you did, but the show will have an interview segment they will use to introduce you. Same for things like this phone call. They will have the sound from both parts of the conversation. You'll see."

The food arrived and Marilyn decided she was starving

"Whose car are you driving. and why the random turns?" Marilyn asked between bites. "I thought I was in a spy movie."

"Babs loaned me her car. Erick's girlfriend couldn't get away tonight. We've been watching the activity around your name on Google. Babs called me to warn me there was a spike just after you sang. Lots of searches on you, pretty much what you'd expect. Only, your song hadn't gone live yet. The spike happened before anybody knew who you were. Babs said it looked like an attempt to tilt the search results by giving more click-throughs to certain kinds of stories."

"So the story's which show a negative side will pop up?"

"That's the weird thing." Anna played with her salad, "They're hitting the positive stories. Someone's priming you to look good. It's not us, so we wondered who?"

"The studio has a lot riding on the show." Tuni pointed a fry at Marilyn. "They can't actually fix the program, but they apparently aren't above trying to give certain contestants a boost. Which leads me to the next question. What are they going to pull next? That's why I suggested we avoid anyone who might be tailing us."

Marilyn looked at her friends, Birungi, Anna and Tuni.

"I pity anyone who goes up against you three. Where did Deanna go? Is she Ok?"

"Someone pulled her aside as they handed you the phone." Birungi said. "We didn't see her after that."

"So we have a week before you get locked into the hotel for the rest of the show." Anna pushed her salad aside. "We'll try to figure what tricks they are going to pull. It's a sure thing they will try to pit friends against each other, but there will be other dramatics as well. This is a new show so we don't know how much behind the scenes stuff they are going to put out. Since you are being kept on a closed campus, I suspect they will show a lot. That means people will be voting on who their favourites are, not just on the singing. It is clear you'll be a nice girl, but you will have to be prepared to be nice in the face of a lot of nastiness from those who choose to play it differently."

"Why would anyone choose to be nasty?" Birungi asked.

"Some people like the nasties. It may be they are seen as more 'real' somehow. Lots of folks just like to stir the pot. Watch for people who are sure they'll be eliminated. They've got nothing to lose."

"Do you think it would be OK to go see Bo?" Marilyn asked.

"You mentioned the Flying Frog on TV," Tuni said. "They'll be packed. Go in the morning before they open. It will make it easier for us to run interference for you if we need to."

Marilyn looked at Anna's salad, her stomach still felt empty.

"Are you going to eat that?"

"No, I ordered it, but don't really want it." Anna pushed it over to Marilyn.

***

The street by the Flying Frog was deserted, so Marilyn hopped out of the car and headed inside.

"Hello." Cher waved at her. "I thought you'd be still sleeping."

"My friends have me on a strict schedule," Marilyn said. "They're predicting something between a slumber party and a riot once we get to this hotel."

"Better you than me, Marilyn." Cher rolled her head and sighed. "You seen Deanna?"

"Not since the audition."

"We could have used her last night," Cher said, "We set up a TV to watch the show in the bar, then all these other people came after you mentioned us. I don't think we'll need to worry about expenses for a while. That's this business, all feast or famine. It's as bad as show business."

"Bo awake?"

"More or less." Cher wiped her eyes. "You go ahead."

Bo hardly made a bump in the blankets, but his eyes lit up when he saw Marilyn.

"You killed them. "Should have known the other girl could sing. I've seen her before somewhere, but you ruled. Just rough enough to be real, but good enough to bring tears to my eyes. What was that bit at the end with your brother? That real?

"Someone told him to call," Marilyn said. "He sounded like Brent. I just got overwhelmed that he called after all these years."

"So why didn't you call him? Bo patted the sheets beside him.

"It's complicated." Marilyn sat and stroked Bo's hand. "He went to my uncle's and refused to talk to either of my parents. I remember Mom crying. They stopped trying for years. One day last year my uncle called Mom. Brent was there and talked to her. They chatted for ages, Mom learned he was married and had a kid. She asked him if he wanted to talk to his sister. He responed he didn't have a sister. He must have gone back over after that because he said he wasn't in the States. Mom and Dad got permission to live on base with his family." Bo patted her leg.

"Family's tough, kid," he left his hand on her thigh, "take it from me, you don't want to drive 'em away, or you'll die like me, alone and bitter."

"You've got Cher," Marilyn said.

"Yeah, me and Cher have a love hate thing going, since she blames me for breaking up her parent's marriage. Not without some cause. She's done Ok by me. When I'm gone, they'll get the other half of this rat trap. Might make things a little easier on them."

Marilyn patted his hand and waited for him to speak again. She looked at him and saw he'd gone to sleep. Gently, she put his hand on his chest and kissed his cheek.

Marilyn gave Cher a hug and left to walk home.

Her phone buzzed just as she walked in the residence.

"Hello,"

"He's gone," Cher said. "I went in to check on him a little while after you left. The old bastard had a smile on his face."

"When will you do the service?"

"He didn't want much, we'll bury him beside his daughter, then come back here."

"When?"

"Day after tomorrow," Cher said. "I don't want it to be a circus. No cameras."

"Keep me posted." Marilyn hung up the phone and walked to Anna's room. Babs answered the door.

"Anna," she called, "Marilyn's here."

"Let her in."

Babs stepped back and Marilyn caught a glimpse of Anna's back as she pulled on a t-shirt.

"I need to cry hysterically, and I don't want to be alone."

"Bo?"

Marilyn managed a nod before the grief flowed out of her. Anna guided her to the bed and sat her down. The sobs were going to tear her in two, but Anna's arms held her together. Someone sat on her other side, and Marilyn felt Birungi's arms holding her too. Tuni came and sat on the floor by her feet. Others came and filled the room, students from class, friends of friends.

Professor Dingman stood in the door. It wasn't enough to hold her together, but they made it safe for her to fall apart.

***

Marilyn woke in Anna's bed sandwiched between Anna and Birungi. A hollow sat beneath her breastbone and her throat ached. The tears started again when she thought that Bo would be mad if she couldn't sing because of him. She let them flow.

"Hey," Anna rolled out of bed. "you're awake. You up for some breakfast? I can bring something up for you."

"Better make it a lot," Tuni said from the floor. She sat up with a grace that made Marilyn smile.

"Is your dancing better too?" Marilyn wiped her tears away with her hands.

"Marginally," Tuni shrugged and smiled briefly. "Yoga is terrific conditioning, but it doesn't help me with a sense of rhythm."

Anna slipped out the door and Marilyn looked at Birungi still sleeping.

"I can't believe you stayed and slept on the floor." Marilyn twisted and stretched. Everything ached.

"I slept on a lot of floors in India. I got used to it."

"Now you're back to real beds."

"*That* is taking some adjusting." Tuni stood up and stretched. "I've given up more than one night and moved to the floor."

"It is true." Birungi sat up and looked around. "It took much practice for me to sleep on the soft mattress. Where is Anna?"

"She went for breakfast," Marilyn said.

"Perhaps she will need help carrying the food." She went out the door.

"You going to be all right?" Tuni sat on the bed and patted the mattress. Marilyn sat beside her.

"Yeah, I'll be all right. I needed to get it out of my system. You being there helped. I can't believe all those people came."

"You've made an impression," Tuni looked up at Marilyn. "It isn't just the singing thing either. You are who you are here."

"That's funny," Marilyn said "Dr. Tripp told me I'd spend my entire life becoming me."

"So, there's hope for me yet."

Marilyn put her arm around Tuni and held her tight.

"I don't know where I'd go," Tuni whispered, "if I needed what you did last night. Who'd hold me together?"

"You'd come to me, and I'd hold you, then Anna would come and Birungi. You're stuck with us now."

Tuni put her head against Marilyn's shoulder.

"You have no idea how much that means to me."

Marilyn didn't feel as hollow now, holding her oldest, dearest friend.
***

"You wouldn't believe the zoo down there," Anna came back from her scouting trip. The media is all over the place. I don't know how we'll get you out of here with them following."

"I'm not going to let them turn Bo's service into a circus."

"Perhaps we need to disguise Marilyn to get her past the media." Birungi said.

"Whatever we are going to do, we'd better do it or she'll be late." Anna paced the floor in frustration.

"I have a suggestion," Erick followed Tuni along the hall. "I owe you for something I did. I will explain later, but Marilyn and I are the same height. I could wear her clothes and lead the reporters away."

"I would work if Birungi and I went with him"

"Won't they notice his face?"

"We put a scarf on it," Birungi took the scarf from her neck and tied it on Erick. Marilyn handed him some clothes and he pulled them on over his own. A rolled up t-shirt gave him a little shape.

"We'll go out the side door on the east," Anna and Birungi led him away down the hall. Tuni led Marilyn the other way. They ran down the stair to the first floor. Tuni pulled her into a room.

"This is Erick's room. He happens to have a window that opens." Tuni picked up a hat from his desk and put it over Marilyn's head. Marilyn tucked as much hair as she could into it while Tuni opened the window.

"We're clear. You got out first, and I'll follow."

Marilyn climbed out the window and waited to help Tuni. She caught her friend and was lifting her down from the window when she heard a shout from behind. Without thinking she wrapped her arms around Tuni and planted a kiss on her.

"Not them."

"Over there!" And footsteps headed away toward where growing confusion rumbled.

Tuni pulled Marilyn in the other direction. They got around the corner and found Erick's girlfriend Tavi waited with the car. They piled into the back and she drove away while Marilyn slouched in the back seat.

Tuni read the directions to the cemetery and Tavi followed them carefully. No one chased after them. They pulled up and parked. Marilyn pulled off the hat and dropped it on the seat. She led Tuni to where the small gathering of people surrounded a hole in the ground.

"Bo didn't want much ceremony." Cher started as soon as Marilyn arrived. "But he knew we'd need to say goodbye. Anyone who wants can share a story, or just a couple of words. Then you can put a shovel of dirt in the hole."

Mack put a wooden box in the hole.

"Bo helped us make a go of the bar. He never really took his share of the profit. Said he didn't need it anymore. He was the most brilliant drummer I ever knew when he was sober, and the most irritating when he was drunk. He was drunk a lot." Mack picked up the shovel and dug into the pile of dirt, then spread the dirt over the box.

"He was my father's best friend. For years, I blamed him for breaking up my family by leading my father astray. Last little while I realized my father made his own decisions, right or wrong. It wasn't Bo's fault. He stepped up to help when my father died, even when he was sure I hated him. I never thought to tell him I forgave him. Sorry Bo." Cher spread dirt on the box.

Person after person told a story, most of them were people Marilyn didn't know. Finally, she was the only one left to speak.

"I waited to be last," Marilyn said, "because I probably knew him the shortest time. He decided to teach me to play the drums after hearing me play one night at the Frog. His teaching method was to be insulting and crude. It was very effective. He didn't just teach me the drums. He taught me about life in the *business* as he called it. He encouraged me, warned me. The last thing he tried to do in this life was feel me up. Bo was an incorrigible, dirty old man and I'm going to miss him. Bo was a musician, so it is only right I send him off with a song."

Breathe in.
Breathe out.
Breathe in.
Sing

-12-

"Right now," the judge said, "this is where it gets serious. There are two hundred of you here, but only forty spots in the live shows where the audience gets to vote."

"You'll have to earn those spots," the second judge said. "We're going to make you work. You'll sing like you've never sung before in different styles and in different ranges."

"We may stop you in the hall and ask for a song." The third judge gave an evil grin as she said her part.

"We don't leave this hotel until we have a winner." The fourth judge flung open the doors and the contestants flooded in.

They had been flown to Las Vegas and driven to the hotel. Once all of them were assembled, the judges had come out to say their piece. It wasn't a huge hotel, but it would hold them all, and it had a ballroom with a stage for them to sing on.

According to the information sheet Marilyn received along with her plane ticket, they weren't to leave the hotel except for dire emergency or when they were eliminated. They would live and compete in the place until the winner was decided. Tickets to the shows were for sale if families wanted to come once the voting shows started.

Marilyn found her room and dropped her bag on the bed. They'd been given an hour to settle in before they started work. The water in the bottle on the side table went down cool and soothing. Her throat still felt a little raspy and tender. They had five days of singing boot camp before they learned if they made it to the voting round. Marilyn suspected being able to perform at a moment's notice would be as important as vocal quality.

Her suitcase wasn't very big. Marilyn brought just a few plain outfits, but Birungi sent dozens of scarves of all colours and moods along with some instructions on how to wear them. She found a brown envelope at the bottom of the suitcase.

Babs found these. They were gone when she tried to show me. Fortunately, she took screen shots. It's up to you what you think you should do with them.

The photos went back a few years. Marilyn recognized Deanna singing at a regional competition, only the caption identified her as Gretta. Another photo of her and a different name. She'd been entering contests for at least six years. Bo had been right. Marilyn thought of the voice that came from Deanna when she sang. The pictures and envelope went in the bottom of her suitcase.

***

"A few housekeeping things," a woman said when they'd gathered in the ball room. "If you have any issues with the hotel. That is, food, your room or plumbing. Call the hotel desk or speak to someone in a hotel uniform. They will help you out. If you have dietary preferences speak to the staff in the dining room and they will do their best. If you have any concerns with the contest, or the show speak to one of us with these name tags. They will have our face and our name. You will be given your name tags in a few minutes. Ours are white, contestant name tags are green. The judge's name tags are gold.

"The judges may ask you to sing at any time. You will have five seconds to prepare yourself and then you will sing for thirty seconds. This contest is all about singing. The judges will not ask you to do anything but sing. If you feel a request is unfair or inappropriate, you may speak to anyone with a white tag and they will direct you to me or Mr. Sminck." She pointed to where he stood leaning against the wall. Marilyn recognized him from the university contest. "After conferring with the judges we'll make a decision.

"Keep in mind this is a TV show. There will be cameras in the hallways and public spaces of the hotel. Your rooms are absolutely private. You are not required to allow any show staff, contestant or judge into your room. We encourage you to maintain those boundaries. Any form of harassment by anyone in the hotel will not be tolerated.

"That brings me to my next point. The show decided it would be too costly to attempt to limit access to the internet, so you have full access to the web in your rooms. There will be a card explaining how to sign on. The rest of the hotel does not have accessible wireless. You may post pictures, video, text, to your blogs or whatever site you wish. If you post anything the show's producers deem to be detrimental to the program it will be removed as will the person who posted it.

"If you have any questions, ask."

Carl Sminck sauntered up to the mic.

"It's my job to make a successful show here. Successful means one people will watch and the sponsors will pay to advertise on. Fake drama is not good TV. Keep it real, keep it about the singing and we will all be successful.

"Now, I want to properly introduce the judges, we have singer song writer Gordon Liller." The first judge stepped through a door behind Carl. "Rapper Even Odds," the other male judge came through the door. "Pop star and record producer Tiffany Dantice" she walked through the door and waved. "Lastly, but not least, opera singer Marguerite Defoult." the final judge walked through the door.

"These are the people who sent you here, but now they are the people who may have to send you home. This is where it gets serious." Carl walked away from the mic and Gordon took over.

"There are tables around the edge of the room." Gordon's voice had a pleasant twang to it. "Your name tags are on those tables laid out in alphabetical order. Find your name tag. On the back of the name tag will be the judge who will be your coach for the next five days. They are going to work to make you look and sound your best. The rest of us will be trying to make you look bad. Go now and find your name then follow your coach to your practice room."

Marilyn headed for a middle table then worked her way around to find her tag. It had a shot of her looking triumphant center stage. A glance at the tags beside her showed similar pictures.

On the back of the tag she saw Even Odds' name and his picture. *This should be interesting*

A crowd milled around each of the judges. Marilyn walked up to her coach.

"Marilyn," he said, "a cappella version of *Dock of the Bay*. I had to fight hard to get you on my team.

"Thanks."

When all the contestants had found their coaches, Even waved at his group to follow and led them through a door and down a hallway. They entered a room that looked like a studio. Speakers surrounded them and instruments filled the corners.

"Welcome to my team," Even grinned at them. "You're here because rap is rhythm and soul. We're not just rap though, so I have a few assistants who are going to help you with learning the instrument that is your voice. There's not one of us in this room who doesn't have to work to improve ourselves."

People with white badges came into the room and stood around the edge of the room.

"Each of my people has a specialty, I'm going to listen to you sing and I'll assign you to a specialist. They'll work with you for the rest of the afternoon. I'll call you up and you'll sing until I tell you to stop. Then I'll point you where you need to go."

"What are we supposed to sing?" a man near the front asked.

"Whatever you want, Colin," Even said, "You may as well start. Don't hurt yourself folks, you have nothing to prove, yet."

Colin sang a country song in a rich baritone. After no more than ten seconds Even pointed him away to the side. A woman stepped up and sang what sounded like opera, she got sent a different way. Marilyn stepped up next and was fifteen seconds into *Me and my Shadow* when she was sent to a corner where a big Korean woman greeted her with a smile.

"We are going to work on projecting your lower register," she said. "Let's get to work. I will give you an exercise to work on until I get back to you..."

At the end of the afternoon Marilyn's stomach muscles ached. She'd never thought breathing would be so much work. They were sent off to dinner with a reminder that any judge could ask them to sing on the spot.

The first victim wasn't out of the food line yet when Gordon tapped him on the shoulder and asked him to sing. He was greeted with cheers and applause when he sang *Food, glorious food.* Several people joined in. Marilyn ran through songs in her head for when she got that tap on the shoulder. When she did she stood up and sang *My Way* in a clear tenor. She got some applause, but after twenty songs, people weren't responding as much.

"After supper we are going to try you out with some harmony." Tiffany announced. "Head to the ball room through those doors."

Chairs waited for them and Marilyn sank into one. Deanna sat beside her.

"How's it going?" Deanna asked.

"Never knew singing would be such hard work."

"They're just getting warmed up," Deanna grimmaced. "Stands to reason the first day will be the easiest.

"Harmony," Marguerite walked to the front of the room, "is essential to good music. Harmony requires you to listen to yourself and another person at the same time. Don't let yourself be distracted. Marilyn." Marguerite pointed to her. Sing. Marilyn cursed, she hadn't been thinking of a song. She started *Feeling Good*, but it was in the wrong key. It would go too low. She pulled everything her coach told her about lower register and sustained the notes. She barely noticed Gordon's tenor join hers. He wove notes above and below hers. Than Marguerite jumped in with an eerie descant that made her teeth ache. Even started a syncopated beat and Tiffany added her own beat. Marguerite waved her to stop.

"Awesome," she said, "Colin, sing." It took all evening to work through each contestant. Some people didn't last the thirty seconds, others got a one word bit of praise. Deanna sang what sounded like a gospel piece.

"Harmony's a blast if you sing in a choir," Deanna whispered after her turn.

"OK, people." Even waved them away. "Off to your rooms. Tomorrow's going to be a long day."

Marilyn showered and changed, then crawled under the covers.

The phone woke her in the morning.

"This is your wake-up call," a cheery girl said. "Breakfast begins in thirty minutes in the dining room."

Marilyn stretched and changed. She put on the first scarf Birungi gave her for luck. A few minutes to send a fast email to her friends and it was time to head to breakfast.

Marguerite was waiting for her in the hallway.

"A song for the morning. Sing."

"Good morning, good morning" Marilyn sang praying the thirty seconds ran out before the words she remembered.

"Nice," Marguerite said before chasing down her next victim. Music came from all directions. There didn't seem to be any pattern to the way the judges chose their victims. Someone was asked to sing three times in as many minutes. Deanna hadn't been tapped yet. Music ran like her ipod on shuffle in Marilyn's head. She loved the jazz numbers but listened to everything. Tiffany tapped her and Marilyn sang one of pop star's own songs back at her. That led to

Tiffany joining in the song and making a complete song and dance out of it. At the end, she put a safety pin on Marilyn's name tag.

"What?" Marilyn started to ask, but Tiffany put her finger to her lips and danced her way to another victim.

The rest of the day they either worked with their coaches or sang in challenges as a group in the ball room. Marilyn started to make her own list of people she thought would make the first cut. Deanna headed the list, and Colin who sang opera with as much ease as country. There was a girl name Alice who looked nervous all the time. Her voice was even purer than Deanna's but she only had a few songs in her repetoire.

"Listen," Deanna said to Alice at lunch, "all I'm saying is if you know a few more songs it will do you good. Everyone else has yet to repeat a song."

"But I know those ones," Alice said, "they're the ones that pop into my head."

Deanna shrugged and went back to her food. Marilyn was going to tell her to just sing what she wanted to when Gordon tapped her.

"Alice. Sing." He stepped back to give her space. She opened her mouth, then closed it. She broke down in tears. Gordon patted her on the shoulder and went to find someone else. Marilyn shifted to comfort her and spotted a smile on Deanna's face.

Marilyn watched the rest of the day. Deanna would whisper advice in some contestant's ear. Sometimes it worked out, mostly it didn't. She encouraged people to stretch out of their comfort zones, but in the pressure cooker of this hotel, moving out of a comfort zone meant disaster more often than triumph.

Before going to bed Marilyn searched the music each of the judges sang and loaded it on her ipod. She'd been lucky with Tiffany. Other people had tried singing the judge's music, but no one else had got a golden pin for it. Colin had two, one for hitting a ridiculously high note in an operatic aria. He got it from Even, not Marguerite. Gordon gave him one for singing something by Elvis. They appeared to be random, so Marilyn stopped worrying. She lay on her bed and listened to music until she fell asleep.

***

Marilyn sat in the ballroom as contestant after contestant was called into the decision room with the judges. No one came back out so she didn't know who made it and who didn't. She'd never been so tired, but she'd learned more than she thought possible in just five days.

"Marilyn," Gordon called her over to the decision room.

"So," Even asked, "if you were a judge, who would you keep?

"Deanna, Colin, me, the little Chinese rapper whose name I can't remember—"

"That's good," Tiffany interrupted her. "It's important to know what the competition is doing. Do you know what that gold pin is?"

"I'm lucky," Marilyn said. "I hit a random thing with my song."

"That's how you got it," Tiffany said. "You kept it by stepping up every time you were asked to sing. What it means is that I've stolen you for my team. Congratulations, you are going to the next round."

Marilyn managed a grin.

"What no song, no dance?" Even asked.

"Give me a night's sleep and I'll give you your song and dance."

"Deal," Even said..

Marilyn went to her room. She texted her friends she was still in. She put the ipod on shuffle and sat listening to music.

Tiffany had commented about watching the competition. She have to think it. Tomorrow.

The phone woke her for breakfast. Marilyn looked at her messages and smiled at the congratulatory notes from her friends.

Even met her at the door of the dining hall with a wicked grin in his eye.

Marilyn grabbed him and sang a children's waltz tune while she spun him around the dining hall.

It echoed with the missing people. Most of the people she expected were there. Deanna waved at her and Colin gave her a thumbs up.

"You have the day off," Even told them after the dance. "Relax, rejuvenate. Get ready for the next round. You made it this far, don't stop now. We'll watch the show in the ballroom after supper." He blew Marilyn a kiss then left the dining room.

Marilyn went back to her room after breakfast, but didn't feel like sleeping. There had to be a weight room in a hotel like this.

The hotel staff showed her the exercise room and Marilyn worked herself into a pleasant sweat. Even after she started on the hormones, she had kept up with Brent's weights. She couldn't bring them to university and she hadn't tracked down the weight room there. An oversight she planned to fix at the first opportunity.

A shower in her room left her buzzing with energy. She decided to go to the practice room and check out some of the gear.

The drum set was the biggest she'd ever seen. Marilyn sat on the stool and picked a song in her head. Her hands began slow with the basic beat, then added some of the riffs Bo taught her. She added more and more rhythm, pushing to find her limit on this immense set.

"Not bad." Even leaned in the doorway. "I wondered who was playing with my gear."

"I haven't played since my teacher died," Marilyn said.

"Well, then, let's give him a proper send off." Even sat at the piano and started playing. Marilyn laid down the rhythm. Like Crysta and her guitar, she followed Even's line and worked to make him sound good. They went through several pieces and Even's grin grew wider after each one.

"Damn, girl," he said when he stopped. "You learned from one fine drummer. You keep working on those sticks and I'll be taking you out on tour with me." He got off the bench and walked over and offered her his hand. She climbed out from behind the drums.

"Do you help all you drummers out?"

"Just the pretty ones," Even winked at her. He led her out and through the hotel to door with Tiffany's face on it.

"Tiffany stole you fair and square," he said, "you got to hang her until I steal you back."

***

They watched themselves sing on command. Everyone moaned at one point or another, but there were high points. Tiffany's dance, and stealing Marilyn. The dining hall singing *Food, Glorious food* They showed a few of the reveals of who was in or out, but not Marilyn's.

"We start the voting shows this week." Marguerite's turn to explain what was coming. "Ten people sing in each show, the bottom five get eliminated. By next weekend you'll be down to half. Then we have the semi-finals and finals, before the top five sing off in a grand finale. We will still be working you during the day, so be sharp. What you do during the day may affect the order you perform. Get a good night's sleep. You'll be working with your coaches to choose your song."

Marilyn went to her room and checked her phone. There were half a dozen messages from Anna, so she called instead of texting.

"Hey," she asked, "what's going on?"

"Some weird postings on the internet. There's some stuff about your days as a thug in school and how horrible you were."

"I *was* horrible."

"Yeah, but we don't want people thinking thug, when they think of you. There's some ugly looking pictures with the stories."

"Probably yearbook," Marilyn said.

"There's some other stuff too, audio of you practicing, bootlegged from the practice room."

"It explains why Erick owed me that favour."

"There's a video of you playing Ophelia in some school play. It's just part of a scene."

"I have to see that." Marilyn's heart skipped a beat. "Can you send me the link?"

"Sure, we're reposting some of your videos, trying to boost your visibility."

"Whatever," Marilyn said. "I need to see that video."

"Ok, the link's gone to you,"

"Sorry, Anna, it's just I didn't even know anyone taped it."

"I understand, Birungi says to bring you greetings. She's gone to dinner with Cameron, but not until after they watched the show. Any problem with Deanna?

"Not serious," Marilyn made herself answer instead of hanging up to look for the link to Ophelia. "She gives people good advice at the wrong time. It may not be deliberate, but she was awfully pleased with herself.

"You got my envelope?"

"Yeah, I don't know, Anna. Is it against the rules to lie in your story? If we push it, it may rebound on us. You said I was the good girl. Let's sit on it for now and see how it goes."

"Fair enough. I'll keep you posted."

Marilyn hung up and clicked on the link Anna sent.

There she was as a young girl, stammering out Shakespeare's poetry but ethereal and beautiful in the white dress. Marilyn watched the scene over and over. It was real. She had been Marilyn even then.

-13-

"Good morning, Marilyn," Carl Sminck sat down beside her at breakfast. "We're doing your follow up interview to play before you sing next. You are giving it a good run for the money, but we need to get your story out to the people who will vote for you."

"A friend found an old video of me as a girl in a play," Marilyn said.

"That was a fortunate find." He smiled toothily. "It's hard to vote against someone a delicate and earnest as that little girl. Perhaps if we find you a white dress to sing in."

"You dug it up?"

"This is a TV show, Marilyn. That means we need ratings. To get ratings we need to have something unusual, unique even. There are so many talent shows, but we are the only one with you. Your story is gripping, heartbreaking. You are my best find. A nudge here, a push there and you'll go far. We need you to make it at least to the finals to get the ratings we projected."

"You're using me."

"And you are using us." Carl met her gaze. "We are the ones who are offering you a chance to escape your life and build the life you want."

"I like the life I have, I just need—"

"More? More money for school, more money for your all-important surgery. More money to travel like your friend Tuni and see the world." He leaned in close to her. "This is your chance for more. Keep that in mind." He got up and wandered off.

Marilyn wanted to run and take a shower. She sat and breathed instead.

"What did the slime bucket want?" Deanna sat down beside her.

"He wants to own me."

"Figures," Deanna looked at the door he left through. "It won't work."

"What won't work?"

"Playing the sob story. Isn't that what he wanted from you? A little more pathos to wring the heart of the voting public."

"How long have you been doing this?"

"I don't know," Deanna looked down. "Really. My earliest memory is of walking on stage. I grew up performing and not quite making it to the top. My mother beat me up at a talent show, so I went into foster care. I'd come third and she wanted the prize money. Even in foster care I kept entering. I knew I would win the next one. Never did."

"So you started cheating?"

"I haven't broken any rules." Deanna glared at Marilyn. "There is no rule against reinventing yourself. You did it."

"I became myself."

"A rough and ugly trip?"

"Yes." Marilyn spread jam on her toast. "I may wish it happened differently, but it is what it is. No different from your story."

"Stay out of my way, Marilyn."

"I'm not in your way."

"Everybody's in my way." Deanna walked off.

Marilyn looked at the toast in her hand, then put it down and went to get ready for the interview.

***

"So, Marilyn, what does it feel like to be a woman in a man's body?"

Nothing like starting off with an easy question.

"I can't speak for other transgendered persons. For me it was like there was another person hiding inside me. She stared at me through the mirror. The first time I saw her was when I put on a dress for a part in a school play."

"This is you?"

A large screen version of Marilyn in the white dress spoke a few lines of Shakespeare then froze.

"Yes." Marilyn wanted to reach into the picture and hug that child and tell her it would be OK.

"And this is what drove a wedge between you and your brother."

"He couldn't understand who I was."

"What are your feelings for you brother now?"

"I love him. I wish he'd been there to help me, but he needed time to come to grips with me being his sister instead of his brother."

"Even if it took seven years?"

"Whatever time it takes. He'll always be my big brother."

"So what got you into music?"

"I've always loved music," Marilyn said. "We had a band even back then. I came through a very dark time in my life and someone reintroduced me to music. It saved my life."

"Why now? Why this contest?"

"My father had a heart attack and it ate up all my parents' savings. They had to sell the house and move to live with my brother. I couldn't tell them not to use my university money. The contest came at the right time and I had friends who encouraged me."

"Good luck."

"Thanks."

***

"I really think this is your best choice," Tiffany frowned at Marilyn.

"It doesn't feel right," Marilyn said.

"You're a girl. The song's about being a girl. What's the problem?"

"The melody sounds ridiculous in a tenor. It comes across more vaudeville than pop."

"Which one do you like?"

"This one," Marilyn held up sheet music. "It's sexy and feminine, but it will work with my lower voice.

"It's your choice," Tiffany sighed and leaned back. "If you get eliminated I'll hate you forever."

"We'd better make this thing work then."

Tiffany worked Marilyn and her team mates on their song choices through the day, popping in and out to make sure she was rehearsing properly.

"Ok, go rest." Tiffany said, "and I mean rest. You're on tonight.

***

Waiting might have been easier than going first. Marilyn didn't notice any maneuvering for order, unless it was punishment for not taking Tiffany's advice. The argument over the song took so much out of Marilyn she didn't argue over wearing the white dress costuming found for her. She wore a gossamer scarf with the dress. The white made her look dead. She forced the makeup people not to overcompensate and make her look like a clown. The tech counted down time before her entry. She could see her interview playing on the screen for the audience. *Fake, I sound fake. There's no passion.*

"Go," the tech tapped her on the arm.

Marilyn didn't want to look; she was dead anyway. This was going to finish her. She pulled the scarf up over her face. The judges looked at each other in puzzlement, shrugging their shoulders. Tiffany sat back and covered her face.

The music started.

Breathe in, breathe in.

Not sing, but *roar.*

The song started in her middle range with moderately strong note. Marilyn made it bounce off the back of the hall at the same time she flipped the scarf back. She caught her first note and sent it back higher clearer. She wasn't going down without a fight.

The audience reacted to the first note and Marilyn wove them into the song and pulled them with her. She was fire and they were tinder. The music lit them up and carried them. She strengthened the beat of the song and made it a dance. Subtle, a bit of leg, a twitch of the hand. The end even bigger than the start. Then drop and three soft high notes. She dropped her head and the scarf fell back over her face.

Applause washed over Marilyn and brought her back, she lifted the scarf from her face and arranged it carefully.

"Opera," Gordon was saying, "you let her sing opera?"

"Bloody brilliant." Marguerite leaned over to look at Tiffany. "I thought you'd lost your mind, but she pulled it off."

"I don't know what you were doing with that first note," Even said. "I'm going to need a wardrobe change."

"What made you choose that song?" Marguerite asked. "I have to know."

"I met Marilyn the first time when I looked in the mirror at the age of twelve. The next five years I spent trying to kill her, but she wouldn't die. Then one day, I just changed and became

Marilyn. Suddenly, I was alive in a way I'd never imagined. Becoming Marilyn saved my life."

"You were right," Tiffany said. "I don't want to admit it, but you were right.

Marilyn walked off the stage as the applause continued then she found a corner and fell into it shaking and gasping.

"You lost it, didn't you?" Deanna sat beside her. "Win or lose, the webbies will be arguing about your performance forever. I've been there. Thought I had nothing to lose and just threw it in their faces. It can make you brilliant, but it takes a steep price." She pulled Marilyn to her feet. "You're better to walk it off. One step at a time."

"Why help me now?"

"Don't know, why not? You did your bit and it's in the can. Nothing I can do but wait and see. We still have three rounds left." Deanna left Marilyn by the stage door.

***

"What kind of stunt was that?" Carl Sminck snarled at her when he found her at the stage door.

"I sang," The hoarseness in her voice covered up the shake.

"If you want to get anywhere, you need to get with the program. People want a sweet kind transgendered girl who sings nice songs. They won't vote for someone who gives them nightmares."

"You're awfully involved in this for someone who isn't involved."

"It's my show," Carl leaned in close to her, "and I will make or break whoever I need to. Decide what you want and do what you're told." He walked away and Marilyn looked up to see Deanna looking at her. The other mimed holding a rope and hanging herself.

***

To save time and keep the show moving they showed people who were moving on at the beginning of the next show. It was quick and brutal. Five names called, *You're in,* to the rest *Goodbye.* Marilyn's performance was the most talked about, but she was third in the voting and moved to the next round.

She didn't find it easier to watch the next shows as people she had begun to know as friends disappeared. The vanished haunted the hotel. Those who were left huddled in corners away from each other.

The voters were fickle and some people left Marilyn was sure would stay. Deanna and Colin each won their round. Lee, the Chinese rapper went home. Charise a tough looking girl rocker stayed.

***

"There's an article alleging your brother was paid to make the call to you. Apparently the military are investigating. Also, some scuttlebutt that Deanna is too slick to be who she says she is. You have the only proof."

"I know, Anna, but she deserves her chance."

"Be careful," Birungi spoke in the background, "I'm afraid of what this is doing to you. That song was very close to your heart."

"You were brilliant," Tuni said. "My heart just about stopped, for more than one reason.

"The semis are next week," Anna said. "Take care of yourself."

-14-

"We are going to have a little fun and mix things up a bit," Gordon announced. The ballroom swallowed the little group of twenty contestants. "We will give you a word and you sing something using that word. Instead of giving you five second to start we'll time how long it takes you to sing. As long as the word is a legitimate lyric the time stops when you start singing."

Marilyn let the song in her head run to a close. She'd need some luck and an uncluttered mind.

"Colin. Balloon." The game started and soon they were laughing at each other's choice of songs. The judges appeared to be laying side bets on the outcomes and their antics were almost as funny as the songs. Distracting too, Marilyn almost missed her name and word being called, but she managed. At the end of the game the judges called out names of people to go and stand with them. Even grinned broadly and Tiffany pouted as he called out Marilyn's name.

"These are your coaches, for now," Gordon said. "We may play more games to pass the time, but for now, go to work.

***

"They're posting YouTube videos of the stuff you're doing," Tuni said on the phone. "You need to smile more. Mostly from what I guess is last week. There are more people around. Anna and Birungi send their love, but they're busy cooking something up. The thing about your brother fizzled. His commanding officer says Brent had permission to make the call and no finances were involved. My year at *New Economy* is almost up, Marilyn, and I need to decide what I'm going to do next. Being smart doesn't translate into being rich. I need some kind of job."

"Stay in Seattle."

"I'll try."

Marilyn hung up and sat in her room. She put a smile on her face. It hung foreign and discordant, but she kept it there until it started feeling natural again.

***

"You want me to sing a rap?"

"Keep surprising people, Marilyn. You nailed the operatic song, you started with a jazzy piece, let's keep it moving."

"I've never tried rap."

"You're a drummer," Even said, "It's like drumming with your voice. All rhythm.

Get with the program Carl's voice grated in her head.

"We'd better get started." Marilyn sighed.

Hours later she was spitting out words and swearing at Even.

"How do you get the words to fit? I can't talk that fast."

"Worry about the rhythm. We can bring it up to speed if you get the rhythm.

Marilyn kept at it. Late in the afternoon a switch flipped in her mind and the words fell into place. They were words talking of loneliness and strength.

"Ok, now the easy part." Even told her. "The bridge."

Singing the bridge was easy, flipping back and forth between the rap and the singing taxed her concentration.

"OK. Even waved her to stop finally. "Let it rest for today. We'll pick it up tomorrow.

Marilyn lay in her bed and tried to play the rap in her head. Instead she heard *Get with the program* and *more, more money to travel - to see Tuni.*

Stuffing the earbuds into her ears, Marilyn found the song she was working on, put it on repeat and let it drown out everything else in her mind.

***

"One last time, Marilyn," Carl said, "work with me and I can get you to the finals, maybe the grand finals."

"I'm doing what I'm told, Carl," Marilyn tried not to snap back at him.

"I need something to work with something showing you as the wonderful, talented transgender you are."

"I'm not just transgendered." Marilyn ground her teeth. "I'm a girl."

"Trust me. I know what sells." He walked off talking into his phone.

Marilyn went back to practice with Even.

The rap just wouldn't come together, but Even didn't want to give up.

"It's too late to work up something else, Even." Marilyn drank a bottle of water letting it wash away the edges of the words.

"Sorry, Marilyn." The rapper slumped his shoulders. Marilyn looked at him for the first time as a person and not a judge who was there to play with her mind. Tattoos ran under his coffee coloured skin like spells. Sweat beaded on him. He'd worked himself as hard as her. She thought he was younger than he looked, vulnerable beneath the look.

She wrapped her arms around him and felt his arms hold her. The strength in his arms steadied her.

"This is on you, now." He said into her hair. "It's in you. You just have to let it out."

He stepped back and turned away. "Do what you have to do." He looked back at her. "You remind me too much of my sister, what she might have been..." He left her alone in the room.

She might as well have teleported to her room; Marilyn didn't remember walking. She picked up her phone and googled Even, she had to dig deep to find the reference to an older brother's suicide. She read the lyrics to his songs and saw the undercurrent of sorrow, but also an unyielding appeal to the strength within. Rap gave him the freedom to send out subliminal encouragement to the people who could hear it.

"I'm ready, Even," she said to the room.

***

Being third meant she didn't have to go first. She waited, pounding the words through her head, then running the soothing smoothness of the bridge across the bruises they left. She'd refused wardrobe's attempt to dress her as a rapper. She wanted to stay Marilyn, at the last second she snatched a hat from a tech.

"I'll give it back, promise."

He shrugged and she walked to her spot to wait the signal to go.

Charisse, who told Marilyn at dinner she was half Lakota, struggled with her song. Her coach had given her a torch song, soft, sultry seductive. Charisse would have been better with the rap

Marilyn had. She sang with fire, and energy. The song was drowning her. The applause turned the knife and the judges, caught up in their role each twisted it harder.

Marilyn saw the despair in Charisse's eyes as she ran from the stage.

"Give me a second," Marilyn said to the tech.

"I can't."

Marilyn caught Charisse and looked her in the eye.

"It isn't over," she said. "It's not."

The other girl shook her head.

"Let someone else deal with it." The tech sounded frantic. "Five seconds and the music is going to start without you.

"Wait until I'm done?" Marilyn pleaded. "Just stay and wait, five minutes."

Charisse nodded, once.

"two, one."

Marilyn threw the hat onto the stage. It hit the mark as the beat began. Marilyn gave the girl a hard hug and strutted onto the stage. The first line started before she got to the mic so she let it pass. She reached the mic and spat out the words as fast and clear as she could make them.

She didn't own them, the judges frowned, the audience shuffled. Marilyn focused her gaze on Even, and gave him the rap. Everything she had, all the passion, she saw in him. She hit the bridge on the note and poured out the slow, sorrowful notes like a balm for the soul. The rap came back too soon and she melded the melody in the words sliding from singing to speaking, from sorrow to anger. Her eyes burned, her throat ached, but she kept the words pouring out until she was done. The backtrack finished before she did.

Don't give up this life, sister.

Flung out harsh, demanding, unyielding into the emptiness.

Marilyn snatched the hat from the floor and put it on and stared at the judges and dared them to do their worst.

The audience applauded, but it was confused, broken. They'd come in halfway through a private conversation and didn't get it.

"I admire your effort, Marilyn," Tiffany said, "but it didn't come together. It was like the song was tearing itself apart."

"That's what it's like to be me," Marilyn said. "That's my life."

"Those are tears on your face," Gordon asked, "What are they about?"

"Someone out there didn't hear soon enough that life is possible. There are people like me on drugs, drinking, cutting themselves because they don't think they have a choice."

"You attempted suicide, didn't you?"

Marilyn held out her wrists like a badge of honour.

"Life is tough, life as transgendered is unspeakably tough, but it is possible."

"You were late hitting your mark." Marguerite scowled at her. "This is about singing, not the dance."

"I had something I needed to do."

"Five seconds before you go on to sing for the chance of a lifetime, and you had something you needed to do?" Marguerite stood and leaned over the table.

"We don't get to choose the timing."

"So what was so important that you missed you mark?"

"I can't tell you that." Marilyn made her voice as flat and definite as she could.

Marguerite sat down and turned her back to her.

Marilyn walked off the stage and Charisse threw her arms around her and sobbed. Marilyn just held the other girl. She saw the tech who owned the hat and tossed it to him. When Charisse let go, Marilyn looked at her and guided her to a private corner of the studio.

"You going to be Ok?"

"Thanks," Charisse said. "I wish I was like you," she pointed to Marilyn's heart, "here. They're going to crucify you for flaunting the rules. You could have told them."

"You are more important than this contest, Charisse. Life is bigger than this. Go, phone someone who loves you."

Charisse ran out of the studio. Marilyn slumped against the wall.

"Listen to me when I'm talking to you."

The slap wasn't hard, but it shocked Marilyn, she tried to back into the wall.

"You missed your mark, you sang fucking *rap*, you mouthed off the judges. Are you trying to lose?" Carl shoved his face into hers and the spit from his words burned her like acid.

"I did what I was told." Marilyn's gut ached, her fists clenched.

He slapped her again.

"Don't get smart with me, freak. You play it my way. You get to go and plead with all your freak friends to get a life. Mess with me and no one will even let you sing karaoke again.

Marilyn pushed him away.

"I'm not a freak."

"As long as you have this, you are." He grabbed her between the legs and squeezed. "I own you. Don't you forget it." He gave her another squeeze and walked away. He pulled out his phone and started muttering.

"You OK?" the tech stood with the hat and a pen in his hand, his phone in the other. "I got it all on video," he said. "You could have his balls on a platter."

"This is show business." Marilyn didn't try to hide the shake in her voice. "Timing is everything." The tech nodded.

"Sign my hat?" He held it out. "I know what you did, and I heard you sing. If I was allowed to vote, you'd have mine."

Marilyn signed the brim of the hat and handed it to the tech.

"Thanks. You'll know when." She walked back to her room and called Tuni.

"Hey," she said when Tuni picked up. "You see my act yet?"

"Were you late for the reason I think you were?" Tuni asked.

"Probably, but I can't say anymore."

"I liked your bit," Tuni said "I understand the being torn in half by what you are. You saved my life, you know."

"He wasn't going to kill you."

"Not just then, after." Tuni's tears came through her voice. "I was in the shower and I'd thought he'd won and I'd found this old razor blade. I remembered the scars you showed me and I couldn't quit when you hadn't. I threw the blade away and never told anyone. Wherever I am, whatever I'm doing. I'm always going to love you. You know that, right?"

"I know. You go find what you need to find. I'll be here."

"Goodbye, Marilyn."

"Goodbye, Tuni."

She'd just hung up when the phone buzzed again.

"Are you alright?" Anna asked. "I saw your song and it killed me. Babs is still crying."

"I'm Ok," Marilyn said. "I have a favour to ask of Babs."

"Sure, let me put her on."

"You are sheer, fucking genius," Babs said and sniffled.

"I think someone is fixing votes on the show. Do you think you and your friends can find out and get proof?"

"We'll blow the bastards out of the water."

"Not yet. If we bring the whole show down, it will ruin everyone. I'm sure it's just for one contestant."

"That bitch, Deanna?"

"Me."

Marilyn pulled up the video of herself as Ophelia on her laptop.

Sorry, kid, you're never going to be in show business.

"So what do you want me to do?" Babs asked.

"I'm going to ask the impossible," Marilyn said. "I want to lose."

"You're still fucking brilliant."

"Thanks, Babs."

"Marilyn." Anna came back on the phone. "I'm sending you a link. I think you need to watch it."

"I will,"

"Take care of yourself."

"I'll do that too."

The phone buzzed a third time as Marilyn looked for the link Anna sent her.

"Marilyn," Birungi said, "the judges did not like you tonight."

"No, they didn't." Marilyn found the link.

"I liked it very much, Cameron says it is effing genius. He has put it on his ipod and sent it to his friends."

"Thanks, Birungi."

"You sound whole." Birungi somehow sent her smile through the phone. "I am glad."

Marilyn tapped the link as Birungi hung up.

I want to put this out there for the brothers and sisters who need this. Charisse said on her video blog. You know who you are. Marilyn saved my life by making me wait five minutes before I bled myself dry. Five minutes, and the world changed and life became possible again. If you're watching this, sister. I'm your new number one. You need something, you ask and its yours. Five minutes. This one's yours sister.

She broke into rap. Marilyn listened through the ears Even gave her. It was beyond brilliant. Charisse sampled the bridge from Marilyn's performance and laid out her feelings and torment without mercy, but the bridge arced over it and seemed to lift the words toward a cry of hope and passion and dedication.

Marilyn listened to it through the tears that splashed on the screen to match the tears on Charisse's face. The rap ended with the line Marilyn ended on and like Marilyn's it had no track behind it.

Don't give up this life, sister.

Marilyn wasn't going to be a star. That didn't matter. Nothing mattered aside from the fact that Charisse chose to stay alive.

***

Even sat down beside Marilyn at breakfast.

"Thank you," he said.

"I'm not much of a rapper." Marilyn drank her juice.

"You're one hell of a person." He kissed the top of her head and walked away.

She spread jam on her toast as Marguerite sat down.

"I saw Charisse's video. Even made me watch it. Why didn't you just tell us?"

"It wasn't my thing to say."

"But Charisse—"

"Charisse has the right," Marilyn said, "It's her story. It's not mine."

"I wouldn't have stopped her," Marguerite said, "I'd have hit my mark. What does that make me?"

"Human," Marilyn took a bite of the toast. She chewed and swallowed, but Marguerite sat like she needed more. "We all are. Don't sell yourself short, Marguerite."

The contestants all found excuses to bump into Marilyn, some offered commiseration on the performance, some admiration for stopping for Charisse.

"What do you think you're doing? Deanna asked. "Still playing the sob story?"

"I have something for you." Marilyn led Deanna to her room and pulled the envelope from the suitcase.

"Here," Marilyn handed it to her. "It's the only proof you aren't Deanna from the farm with twelve sibling and parents who disowned you."

"What are you going to do with it?"

"I'm giving it to you."

"Why?" Deanna crumpled the envelope in her hands, "You could destroy me with this."

"I don't want to destroy you. I love your voice. The business does strange things to people, Deanna. Be careful it doesn't ruin you, but I want you to have your chance. You deserve it even if you don't believe it."

Deanna ran from the room.

Marilyn watched the video of herself as Ophelia again.

I think I'm getting it, now, Dr. Tripp. Forever becoming me.

Her phone buzzed.

"Marilyn," Anna said, "Ms. Chisolm called me. She was very apologetic, but they can't leave your stuff in your room without payment of the next term's rent. I don't have enough to cover it."

"It's OK, Anna. Clear my stuff out and stash it somewhere. I don't have a lot anyway. Maybe the Flying Frog will store it."

"I called Tuni, but she's not in Seattle anymore."

"I know," Marilyn said, "we talked. She has her own struggles. She'll be back."

"Babs is waging war at her computer, Birungi is off with Cameron. There's nothing I can do."

"Sometimes there is nothing," Marilyn said, "but there *is* something you can do for me, clear out my room. Take care of my stuff."

"But you'll have nowhere to live!"

"I'll find a place."

"Ok," Anna audibly gulped back tears. "If that's what you want."

"Thanks, Anna."

Marilyn hung up. She expected to be terrified now she was officially homeless. She played Charisse's rap again. There were worse things.

-15-

The audience buzzed as the show started. Marilyn sat with the other nine contestants from the first semi-final. Charisse had her fire back, she reached over and clasped Marilyn's hand.

"I saw your video," Marilyn said, "to quote a friend, it's effing brilliant."

Charisse smiled and squeezed Marilyn's hand tighter.

The judges took turns announcing the results. *Don't let me win.* One, two, three, four people stood and waved in victory. Then confusion as the judges argued over the fifth place result.

"We have a tie for fifth place," Gordon announced. "Charisse and Marilyn have exactly the same number of votes. The judges will make the decision. If the rest of you will clear the stage." The audience shouted names at the judges. While the contestants walked away, winners to the right, the others to the left.

Marilyn held tight to Charisse. *Don't let me win*

"You're brilliant, Marilyn," Tiffany said, "and you know I love you, but I have to go with my girl Charisse."

"You struggled with the rap, Marilyn." Gordon sat back and looked at her. "But Charisse didn't do any better with her song. I think Marilyn is the stronger contestant. I'm voting for Marilyn."

"You can't make me chose between these two incredible women." Marguerite sobbed. "I can't do it. Sorry, I just can't."

Marilyn breathed in deep, and spoke before Even could.

"Let Charisse go through."

Charisse spun and looked at Marilyn wide-eyed as the audience screamed louder.

Even waved for silence.

"You know Marilyn is on my team," he said, "and I have to back up my team mate." He left his seat and walked up on stage. He hugged Charisse. "You are brilliant, darling." He didn't say anything to Marilyn. Wrapping his arms around her he held her until the only thing she knew was his heart beat. The entire theatre fell silent as he kissed her on the lips then turned with his arm still around her.

"Charisse is in." He didn't let Marilyn walk to the side of the stage. Instead he walked her through the audience which screamed and clapped and whistled. The ushers opened the door and Even handed her to a man in a black suit.

"This is my driver, John. He's going to make sure you get home." He turned and went back into the theatre.

Marilyn led John to her room and picked up her bag.

"Let's go," she said.

"Where to?"

"There's an army base in Texas. We'll start with that."

John nodded and led her to a long black limousine.

"It will be a long drive, make yourself comfortable."

Marilyn texted her friends.

Going to Texas. Back as soon as I can.

Then she phoned her parents.

"I'm coming home," she said, "I need directions." John stopped while he took notes, then started off again. Marilyn turned her phone off. The world would have to manage without her for a while.

***

Early evening, two days after they left the show, John wheeled the limousine onto a street of houses on the base outside Austin. Nothing moved as they pulled up in front of a house which looked just like the rest.

"This is it, Marilyn." John got out and opened her door then carried the bag to the door. Marilyn rang the doorbell and waited. The air pulled the moisture from her skin and she wished for her water bottle. The door opened and a man in full dress uniform stood there.

"We saw the show. My commanding officer decided I should be here to welcome my sister home." Brent saluted her, then swept her up in a hug. "I am so proud of you." He crushed her to him. "So proud." When he put her down, she turned to thank John, but he and the car were already gone.

"Come on in and meet my family," Brent pulled her in and closed the door.

***

Christmas morning dawned bright and cool. Marilyn stretched and dressed to go downstairs for coffee. Space was tight in the house, but they managed. Her parents took up the basement. Robert had his own room for his toys. Marilyn slept in the baby's room. Brent and Tammy were already up. He had toast and coffee in front of him while Tammy fed Liz.

"Some mail came for you," Brent said. "Marked don't open until Christmas." He passed some envelopes across to her. The sounds of tearing paper and excitement came from the living room where her Mom and Dad watched Robert open his presents.

She ripped the first one open,

It was quite a ride. Colin's note read, *Glad you were a part of it. Merry Christmas wherever you are.* A copy of his new CD was in the envelope. He'd weathered the scandal of Carl's arrest for fraud, assault and a slew of other charges. The company had distanced themselves from Carl, but public opinion forced them to honor the contract with the winner once it was clear the vote fixing ended with Marilyn's exit.

The next one was from Even, front row tickets to a show on New Year's in Las Vegas fell out. He'd circled the small print *Opening Act "Charisse"*. There was a note too.

Where ever you are, whoever you want to bring. I'll make it happen.

The third card had the logo from the Flying Frog on it. When she tore it open, several envelopes fell out. The first was a fat letter from a law firm.

It was Bo's wish that you be able to finish your schooling regardless of other events. To that end he has instructed us to deposit one hundred thousand dollars in an account to cover your expenses while you pursue your degree. When you graduate, the remainder will form the basis for a bursary with terms you define as appropriate for whatever goal you wish to accomplish. Please contact us at your earliest convenience. The university has been informed and has renewed your enrollment for when you are ready to return to study.

The note from Mack was short.

You'll always have place here.

There were cards from Anna and Birungi wishing her a Merry Christmas. A note from Tuni saying she was at a university in New York City.

Marilyn pulled out her phone and texted them.

See you soon, don't make plans for New Year's

The phone buzzed as soon as she hit send. Someone was up early. She checked the message, but it wasn't from either Anna or Birungi.

Check it out. Deanna.

Marilyn tapped the link under the message. It took her to a video.

Hi, my name is Deanna, I've had a bunch of other names too, but I'm sticking with Deanna. I'm a talent show addict. You've seen me recently but I was here, a picture flashed on the screen and here too, another picture. I desperately wanted to win the big show. So desperate I tried to become someone else and became a person I didn't like. A friend believed in me beyond anything I imagined. She let me choose. You know I didn't win, a fantastic musician won and he deserved it. I'm going to try for a different kind of win - giving up talent shows. I'm going to sing and let it be just the music. That's the name of my new channel "Just singing." Every week I post a new song, you'll know I haven't entered a contest. You don't need to vote for me, like me or anything, but if you let me know you're listening it would mean the world. This first song then, is for you, you know who you are.

She started to sing and Marilyn sang along.

"Friend of yours?" Brent asked, "She's got a nice voice."

I'm here, always. M. She hit send.

"You OK, Sis?" Brent put his hand on hers.

"Yeah." Marilyn soaked in the warmth of her brother's hand. "I am."

Other books by Alex

Cry of the White Moose
The Regent's Reign
Calliope and the Sea Serpent
Wendigo Whispers
The Devil Reversed
Generation Gap
The Gods Above
Tales of Light and Dark
Like Mushrooms
The Heronmaster
Blood and Sparkles, and other stories
Princess of Boring
By the Book
Sarcasm is My Superpower
Playing on Yggdrasil
The Unenchanted Princess

Alex also has stories in:
Song of the Axe
Words on the Rocks
Beyond the Wail
Collidor Stream Collection 2016
Read short stories and excerpts from his novels at alexmcgilvery.com